P'THOK CHRONICLES

Tales of the Terran Confederacy

Ralts Bloodthorne

Wordborg Literature

Copyright © 2021 Ralts Bloodthorne

All rights reserved

The characters and events portrayed in this book are fictitious. Any similarity to real persons, living or dead, is coincidental and not intended by the author.

No part of this book may be reproduced, or stored in a retrieval system, or transmitted in any form or by any means, electronic, mechanical, photocopying, recording, or otherwise, without express written permission of the publisher.

ISBN-13: 9781234567890
ISBN-10: 1477123456

Cover design by: Rayebug

For: Heather, Kathy, Maggie, Morgan, Dead, and Hambone.

For being with me through all this.

And everyone on Reddit and Royal Road who encouraged me.

It's obviously bullshit but it's cool, so I choose to believe it.

ANCIENT TERRAN SAYING

P'Thok Eats an Ice Cream Cone

P'Thok carefully unwrapped himself from the clutching confines of his ceramic dropshell, moving his limbs carefully so as not to crack the shell or damage any of the precious equipment that might have survived the perilous drop into the heart of the enemy's home world. He would need the maps, the recorders, and the Terran Republic cash sticks that had been collected from dead Terran soldiers off the battlefield. He would need the counterfeited equipment of a Manti tourist, and some of the special equipment hidden in the harness he would need to wear would allow him to emulate a Manti to any and all sensors with the notable exception of Terran biological optics.

The energetic and youthful yellow sun high in the strangely blue sky warmed P'Thok's carapace, making him feel more awake, more alive than he would normally have felt after a 18 month cold-drift to the enemy home world of the TerraSol Republic, the home world of the only intelligent primate predator in the known universe. With their warlike ways, innovativeness at devising war material, and fearsomeness on the field of battle, P'Thok was slightly surprised that he was even alive, not burned down by the extensive planetary and air defense systems the Terrans possessed. All known species referred to the TerraSol System as "Fortress Sol" due to the heavy defenses.

P'Thok knew he was lucky. He had made it to the surface of Terra itself! He was not drowned in one of those scattered oceans, and not killed by a fast moving piece of space dust puncturing his drop pod, nor did his grav-repulsers malfunction and smear him across one of the fractured pieces of the protocontinent.

Looking carefully around, his vision enhanced by his disguised combat visor, P'Thok saw why he had not been shot down or incinerated by one of those massive weapons emplacements that Hive Intelligence believed covered the entire surface of TerraSol. He was at the edge of one of the huge facilities Terrans seemed to be obsessed with creating, the massive bulk of weapons, and the huge, hulking shapes of Terran warships were everywhere to the magnetic North of P'Thok. East and West were strips of light forest, nice for aesthetic reasons and producing oxygen, if you breathed it. P'Thok enjoyed the sweet smell of Nitrogen that permeated the atmosphere in undreamed of quantities. No wonder the Terran mammals fought so hard to protect their home world, the very air nourished normal intelligent life! P'Thok wondered at the sweet atmosphere, reaching into the pod and pressing the autodestruct sequence. With a hiss, the pod shivered and collapsed into dust that stirred in the sweet-smelling breeze from the huge metropolis to the South of P'Thok's landing site. P'Thok activated his recorders and began moving South, toward the large city that the Treana'ad High Matrons and War Queens had named "Ninth Swarming Place of Furless Mammals" and the Terrans called "New Angelos".

By the time the warm yellow sun had crested its zenith and began moving toward the horizon, P'Thok had been picked up by a well-meaning, nearly polite Terran, and given a ride on the back of a fearsomely fast 2-wheeled transport that roared and shivered and moved like some kind of reptile in and out of the ground-effect vehicle traffic. The talkative mammal had mistaken him for one of the traitorous Manti, one of the mammal's allied races, who had missed something called a "bus". The mammal had given him a ride all the way into the center of the huge metropolis, dropping him off in the center market to do some "sightseeing". The two words meant the same to P'Thok, and he wondered exactly what vision visioning could hold for a tourist to TerraSol as he wandered the spacious streets of the city. Looking around, P'Thok felt his mind reel as he looked up at the huge buildings, some of them taller than the Hive P'Thok had grown from a larvae. Terran's were everywhere, moving about rapidly, and grunting at one another in Terran Standard. To P'Thok the language sounded just as brutal as the Terran's themselves.

The ground vibrated underneath the city, and P'Thok

barely kept his cool, nearly screaming aloud as the very ground shook beneath his feet. Some of the beings around him stared, and P'Thok heard more than one instance of the brutish sound P'Thok knew served as Terran laughter. He could not believe it, the Terran's took no notice of planet instability. That would enable them to live on more planetary bodies than anyone had ever thought! That knowledge alone would guarantee that the Hive Mothers would be pleased with P'Thok's performance. No wonder the mammals fought like the insane, they came from a planet that was just as unstable as they were!

He took pictures carefully, making sure nobeing could see his actions as he recorded both the buildings and the masses of beings that hurried about their business. He was careful to record the mammals entering buildings in great detail. In one instance, P'Thok carefully recorded every available sight of a place that turned away any who were not Terran military. He wondered what the facility, named Harv's Bar and Grill, could possibly be. Weapons research? Strategy planning? Cybernetics or power armor manufacturing. Fluttering his vestigial wings in agitation, P'Thok reluctantly moved away from the tempting building, whose optic-catching holo's seemed almost to try to lure him inside. His sensitive audio receptors, boosted by his head covering, could detect the barking sound of Terran laughter, the sound of glass on glass, glass on plastic, plastic on plastic, and both glass and plastic on metal. Whatever activity was happening inside was plainly quite exciting to the Terrans inside, but the two huge, hulking Terran soldiers on either side of the door intimidated P'Thok to the point he would not even try to peer inside the brightly lit window.

By nearly sunset, P'Thok was beginning to become nervous as he wanted the streets of the gigantic habitation complex. All around him beings were moving about, and on some corners, beings nervously hocked wares to reluctant appearing beings. More than once a male or female Terran would approach another Terran, and they would leave together to enter a building. While he often saw the same being who waited to be approached, he rarely saw the one who made the approach again. Some beings were beginning to stare, and P'Thok became sure that sooner or later, somebeing would recognize he was a Traena'ad instead of a Manti, and the military would be called in to take him into custody. He knew that if the Terrans took him prisoner, he would be cooked over hot liquid vapor, cracked open, and eaten with sauce. Every Traena'ad knew that was what the Terran's did with captured Traena'ad, and P'Thok had seen Terrans dismember, deshell, and devour reddish, exoskeleton clad creatures whose forward digits ended in claws. To P'Thok's horror, he had seen more than one feeding establishment with the lifeforms caged in transparent cells, filled with salinated water, to be picked out by one of the Terrans, and then, after a suitable wait, devoured. P'Thok shivered and tried to think of a way to avoid notice and possible devouring.

Quickly looking around, P'Thok saw quite a few beings purchasing the wares of a stand marked "Ice Cream" in Terran Standard and took note of the fact that nobeing seemed to take notice of any being that devoured the ware. He recorded the stand, including spectrograph analysis, electromagnetic scan and full visual. He worked up his courage and approached, his senses picking up a rich mixture of complex protein chemicals emanating from the cart. Curious, P'Thok stood in line and eventually reached the front of the line, drawing closer and closer to the source of those wonderful airborne scents.

One of the squat bulky mammals was offering a cold semisolid, topping a wrapped breadlike wafer substance. His hairless face was contorted into what Hivehome Intelligence had briefed P'Thok was the equivalent of a smile. To P'Thok, it looked like a gestured intention of imminent devouring, with the bared meat tearing teeth of one of the galaxy's few intelligent predators. P'Thok had seen that expression all day, however, and was past the initial flinching stage that he had been in when first confronted by a grimacing mammal.

"Ice cream, gentlebeing? I have chocolate, raspberry, strawberry, mint chocolate chip, or vanilla left." the man told P'Thok, speaking in rapid Galactic Standard heavily accented with the brutish Terran tones.

"Strawberry." P'Thok half mused, holding out the Terran credit chip. The man scanned the chip, nodded, then scooped out a chunk of pinkish, frosted material and deposited on the open end of the conically wrapped wafer. The Terran handed P'Thok the credit chip and the cone, then waved P'Thok on. The insect warrior moved on, gently testing the cold substance with antenna and equipment, searching to make sure that it was not some type of poison, a mild organic corrosive for cleaning teeth, or a cruel Terran joke that would suddenly eviscerate him in broad daylight in the middle to the street.

Complex carbohydrates, frozen H2O, sweetened wafer, no synthetics. It was safe for consumption, and P'Thok sliced a piece off with one mandible, drawing the rapidly melting piece into his maw. Melted nicely, and the taste reminded P'Thok of fruit, his favorite dish. The cone was not bad either, kind of tuber taste to it. Almost eagerly, he took one more bite, to see if it was as good the second time he ingested the strange substance.

The taste seemed to explode in P'Thok's brain, and he found himself steadily devouring the strange creation. Some beings looked at him but turned away smiling that normally terrifying Terran smile. P'Thok could not care less what other beings did, as long as he had some of this wonderful substance to consume! Here was a creation worth going to war with the Terrans all over again, a secret that showed just how treacherous the mammals were in not sharing it with the all-powerful Traena'ad Hiveworlds, did the stupid little mammals not know that the Traena'ad were Gods, and P'Thok was the most powerful of them all! He found himself dancing quickly, ignored by passerby, and stopped suddenly, a realization dawning on him.

He was invisible! Nobody paid any attention to him. He was invincible! That's why no one dared confront him! P'Thok looked around slyly with the last realization, searching for a female Traena'ad, or even a Manti. After all, he was SEXY. No female would be able to resist him. Even the Terran females were glancing at him slyly, and for a long moment, P'Thok was tempted to trying a cross-species sexual encounter but changed his mind at the sight of their powerful arms and thick, killing digits.

The lights of the city were bright, and seemed to emit sounds of their own, turning the city into a sparkling orchestra of sounds that P'Thok had never imagined in his life! All of the beings he met were friendly toward him, trying to cull the favor of the powerful and wise P'Thok, and even the Terrans seemed acceptable, now that he no longer had to fear them, since we was invisible, omnipotent and irresistible.

All too soon, though, P'Thok began worrying that he had forgotten something. Had he revealed himself to some being he should not have? Had he dropped a piece of equipment that would give him away as a Traena'ad? Had he offended that large Terran cyborg waiting on the corner with a military carry-all in his large, killing hand? Had he forgotten the correct steps for the recreational mating dance?

Dejectedly, he began searching for a place to spend the night, but the huge, friendly city now seemed to distain him, until he moved into a small, cluttered side street and huddled up next to a large, smelly container that was cold and surrounded by slimy refuse. As liquid H2O began falling from the sky, he curled into a ball, miserable with the thought he might have forgotten something that the Hivemothers wanted and lamenting the fact that no females found his pheromones attractive. Sleep came slowly and fitfully, and he dreamed of the Terran military cyborgs that he had seen on the streets chasing him through the tunnels of his Hivehome.

When P'Thok awoke, he discovered some lousy mammal had stolen his foot coverings and rations! Not only was he wet and cold, but he no longer had food that was safe to consume, and his delicate footpads would be subject to whatever horrors the Terrans could devise! Fortunately, he still had most of his equipment, and the credsticks hidden away. He rubbed his vestigial wings together as he decided that the only recourse he had was to purchase some ice cream to eat, or starve.

The passerby for the most part ignored P'Thok for the next several days, as he spent all of his money on the delectable substance known as ice cream, trying as many different types as possible. He could not believe that the Terran's had devised so many distinct flavors! What geniuses! Surely the Hive Mothers would relent and grant the mammals honored being status in the Hive if they would just share the wonderful recipe of delightful concoction with the Traena'ad. Soon, P'Thok began selling some of his non-essential equipment to a man on a corner by a house with friendly Terran women who had lots of visitors at night. Soon, the man began trading the wonderful substance to simply record P'Thok speaking about life in the Hive, while two huge Terrans, nearly entirely mechanical, they were so heavily augmented with cybernetics, guarded P'Thok from the shadowy foes that sought to bring him down. Despite P'Thok's nervousness about the two fearsome combat cyborgs, the friendly man assured P'Thok that they were deserters from the Terran military that believed that Terrans and Traena'ad should work together.

P'Thok could not believe that a simple street vendor sold something that would make the Warrior Caste of the Traena'ad appear harmless to the surrounding Terrans and tourists. Nearly as good as the legends of invisibility! And here was a fool who gave the substance for answers even a larvae would know. What fools these Terrans were. No, not fools, they knew who he was, and they would come and get him soon! Those two 'bodyguards' were in fact Terran military, who were measuring P'Thok for a steaming pot and determining what kind of sauce he would taste good coated with and dipped in!!

Almost clacking with anxiety, P'Thok hurried to the nearest space port, keeping a whole box of ice cream close at hand the whole way, and boarded a flight to the Disputed Zone. There, he ordered his freezer stocked full with as many different types of ice cream as he could order. He really wanted to avoid leaving his room, after all, they were out there, waiting to get him, to keep him from breeding with fertile virgins.

The whole way to the Disputed Zone, nobody even suspected the Traena'ad warrior who ate nothing but ice cream and rubbed it's legs together in glee one moment and whose antennae trembled with fear that they had almost caught him. No one knew that instead of a harmless Manti, peaceful ally of the Terrans, a Traena'ad warrior, a feared infiltrator to the very cradle of Terrans itself, was among them. Had not the Traena'ad defeated the Terran military in 28.83% of all engagements? Had P'Thok himself done something no other had ever done, visited the Terran home world and survived? Wasn't that man by large artificial pond of liquid H2O one of the men who had asked him harmless questions? What exactly was Rocky Road? There was not any chunks of stone, nor did it have any roads in it.

The Disputed Planet Tk'Ktak/Decarus was easy to reach, and easier to move from the Terran occupied areas to the small section of the protocontinent that the Traena'ad still occupied. Before P'Thok left the Terran Occupied Zone, he stole a large, armored ice cream transport vehicle that had specially outfitted to transport the wonderful material. The camouflage built into the vehicle and the bobbing head of a large Terran with a bright red nose and strangely multi-colored hair ensured that none of the Terrans would try to stop P'Thok as he raced out of the Terran Occupied Zone. The severed head atop the vehicle cackled the harsh Terran laughter the entire way, striking fear into everyone, but strangely enough, attracting Terran larvae, who tried to flag P'Thok down with credsticks.

Each crowd of Terran larvae made P'Thok chitter in terror and reach into the back of the armored transport for another ice cream bar. He was deathly afraid the small, voracious creatures would manage to stop his armored vehicle and devour him in a larval feeding frenzy. The vicous little larvae were in such a feeding frenzy that they chased him on their large, crushing feet for long distances, their hunting cries loud as they pursued him.

He was keening in relief when he finally reached the Traena'ad Occupied Zone, pursued by dozens of Terran assault craft who seemed desperate to regain the armored transports valuable cargo intact, and because of that, could not bring their heavy weaponry to bear. Despite that, the ferocity of the Terran assault troops forced what small, remaining forces the Traena'ad had off the planet within hours.

But P'Thok and his invaluable cargo had made it, and once his superiors had sampled the contents of the armored cargo vehicle, they agreed that the loss of a minor planet was nothing compared to the importance of P'Thok's discovery. While sampling the prize P'Thok had returned with, Clutch Leaders decided that they would use their secret weapon, and the invincibility that it bestowed upon them, on the hotly contested world of Chtick'vik, where the Terrans had recently inserted a full Clutch of Terran Heavy Assault Marines.

P'Thok's superiors viewed what tapes P'Thok had not sold off, and agreed, with ice cream in their possession, the mighty Terrans would suffer the fate of any other primate that dared resist a Traena'ad.

Defeat, death, and devouring.

P'Thok and the other warriors gathered together to charge the Terran lines. Their weapons were slung as they moved slowly forward through the line, each of them being handed an ice cream cone by the Clutch Leader. All present were trembling in anticipation of the substance that would turn them from the universes lowest form of life, not fit to even gaze upon the stars, much less travel them, to the greatest thing the universe had ever created, the sum of all that was good, wise, clever, sexy, and powerful.

They had seen what happened to the Terran Marines stationed nearby as the Traena'ad sympathizers stole each ice cream shipment as it came through. Snagging it right from the Terran Naval transports when they touched down, and leaving boxes full of dirt in the place of the crated refrigeration units the ice cream was shipped in. As the ice cream was stolen, the Traena'ad watched the Terrans closely to see what effect it would have on the Terran warriors. More and more fighting among brood brothers, lack of equipment maintenance, lackluster patrols, a complete falling apart of discipline in a force feared galaxy wide for their discipline and ferocity. The Terrans went from almost machinelike to a clutch of larvae without Hivemind touch for guidance.

P'Thok's superiors were pleased with P'Thok's discovery of the secret to Terran ferocity and ability to become nearly invisible anywhere. Not to mention the ability to breed like some kind of scavengers infesting a giant corpse. They had planned in lengthy conferences, partaking of the wondrous substance P'Thok had discovered, and finally settling on the morning's operation. During the long trip, having gotten lost several times, they had devoured the cargo of the armored transport, and so, had to choose a random world to test the power of ice cream on. Wisely, the Clutch Lord had pointed at the map, membranes over his eyes, and stated that that world would be the first to fall.

Each Traena'ad left the bunker complexes that had been their home, scuttling forward on powerful legs, holding the ice cream cones high overhead to grant them invisibility and fearsome combat discipline and skill. Many of the cones were half eaten, and more than one warrior held an empty hand high into the air, snickering to himself with his cleverness at deceiving his superiors into thinking he had not eaten his issued cone.

They drew closer and closer to the Terran lines, not a single shot being fired at them. They could feel a surge of victory as they drew ever closer, soon able to see the Terran Marines staring at them in fear and confusion. Elation filled their hearts as they drew ever closer, coming closer than anyone ever had without being discovered and fired on by the fearsome mammals. Some of the Terrans were bent over, convulsing in terror and their diaphragms spasming so they uttered sharp barks of fear and chagrin.

"Open fire!" one of the Terran's bellowed, and the fearsome firepower of the Terran Marines tore the attacking insect warriors apart. Some of them managed to stagger within spitting distance of the Terrans, but none of them ever fired a rifle, one warrior stopping between two marines to dance and preen at them, displaying his invisibility and cleverness. P'Thok watched the demise of his comrades from behind the boulder where he had stopped to eat his cone, and any cones within reach, and felt sad, but oh well, more would be hatched to replace them. P'Thok figured he would go back and tell Hive Intelligence what had happened.

As soon as he finished this ice cream cone. And maybe the bucket of ice cream in the bunker.

P'Thok Smokes a Pack

The small trader only weighed a handful of megatons, with the standard sextant of jump-drives in the rear section, vast cargo holds (for its size), and a bridge and crew quarters jammed into the nose. It was of Terran make, its transponder squeaking a Terran code, and its drive signatures were on file as being from an older space trading corporation. While it was unusual to see civilian vessels this close to Treana'ad Space, it wasn't unheard of, since war zones could bring profit to the daring. The vessel looked a little weird, and the computer control was hard to understand, but the station chalked it up to the vessel's age and upkeep.

The space station control gave permission for the small craft to dock at one of the main umbilicals and relaxed. There wasn't anything to worry about. It did pause for a moment, the computer system claiming it had to reorient, that a hiccup made it slightly confused on the precise maneuvering required to dock.

That wasn't unusual, traders, even Terran traders, weren't exactly known for their upkeep, so the station wasn't worried as the trader paused, slowly rolling then turning in space to reorient itself on the stellar mass at the center of the system.

P'Thok was a warrior caste Treana'ad of some experience. He had infiltrated Terra-Sol itself and pulled off a daring daylight heist of an armored transport on a Terran rim world, even taken part in two successful military campaigns against the Terrans.

Which is why he had no fear as he engaged the thrusters of his exo-pack, oriented himself, and jetted toward the space station. He had practiced in virtual reality until he no longer felt fear at the idea of drifting across nearly ten miles of vacuum, aiming for a small point on the space station.

It helped that the Matron aboard the craft, who was overseeing the delicate military operation, code named 'I'll Take That', had flooded the warrior's senses with pheromones to instill courage and remove fear.

Still, P'Thok was the only Treana'ad warrior of the ten man assault force not to feel fear. After all, he had escaped a pursuit by literally dozens of Terran larvae during his daring heist two years before, why would he fear a space-walk.

Time moved slowly as P'Thok, clad in stealth armor, coasted toward the station. His bladearms were sharp and honed, his hands gripped a well maintained plasma rifle, and his armored vac-suit was capable of shrugging all but military grade Terran weapons. He had faith in his stealth equipment, after all, it had worked for him to land on Terra itself.

Eventually he reached the space station, throwing out a magnetic grapple on a plas cable. IT only took two tries for him to latch it and he reeled himself in, his squad mates following him. When they landed they activated the magnetic boots and moves slowly across the surface of the station toward their goal. While graviton boots would have been more reliable and easier to use they might have been detected by the stations graviton sensors, the same reason the exo-packs had used compressed atmosphere rather than graviton.

P'Thok reached the target first. A hyper-comm relay, which could be used to alert any nearby military forces to the fact the Treana'ad had arrived to take control of the station. P'Thok carefully opened the relay's control panel and moved aside for D'Rok to disable the hypercom's output mechanism while still allowing incoming transmissions.

Once that was done, the group moved through the silence of space to the next target. Although they all felt nervous, keeping an eye on their atmosphere, they quickly disabled all eight of the automated weapons emplacements, simply cutting the command lines, that way they would react to diagnostic requests and show green but were unable to actually be used for defending the station.

That left one target.

The most important.

Once they had arrived at the target, P'Thok faced the ship and flashed his suit lights four times, letting the ship know that it could stop with the masquerade and dock. The ship flashed its lights once and reoriented to make dock at the docking spindle.

P'Thok entered the airlock with his squad and cycled it, the system already disabled so that the main computer would have no idea the airlock was being used.

The nitrogen was low, almost non-existent, and P'Thok shook his head. His men would have to remain suited, but that was expected. He made motioned, reminding his men not to use radio, and led his two subordinates toward his goal while the other two leaders led their teams toward their objectives.

The station had no idea that P'Thok was even on board. The first hint that Harry Susan Dendles had was when the door opened and the huge armored insectiod stepped into the control office and threw a stun grenade. The Treana'ad didn't move through executing everyone, instead used heavy cargo straps to tie the humans down.

"Which one of you is the station commander?" P'Thok asked, trusting his translator.

"Me," Harry said from the floor, where he'd been virtually mummy wrapped by the Treana'ad, who were taking no chances with the legendary primate strength.

"Bring him," P'Thok ordered.

"Can I ask where?" Harry asked, visions of being roasted over a fire and eaten dancing in his mind.

"I have questions to ask you," P'Thok asked. Personally, he was glad he was in armor. He could see the status of the other members of his squad and see that their stress pheromones were high.

The Matron's blessing must be wearing off. He changed channels to talk to his men. "Flush your pheromones, I don't want you to become overly anxious or aggressive," P'Thok ordered. Each one flashed an assent over their armor and he watched as their anxiety levels dropped.

Being trapped with one's own pheromones could cause problems.

His armor suddenly updated with a map of the station and

P'Thok knew that D'Rok had managed to hack into the station's computer core. He led the human to his own office as his two men carried the properly trussed up human. Once inside he motioned at his two men to put the human in his chair.

At first the bindings posed a problem, as the human was stuck at full body extension. Since the straps were wound all around his body, unwinding the ones around his waist meant undoing some of the windings around his arms or legs. After a moment K'Lana'at looked up.

"Um, sir, we can't undo the straps," the Treana'ad warrior said.

P'Thok sighed, filling his suit with the smell of frustration. Luckily, he'd learned a bit about humans when he had valiantly infiltrated Terra.

"If you give me your word not to 'be stupid', to use your phrase, I'll untie you," P'Thok said. He saw the atmosphere was steadying out and opened his face shield.

The human nodded. "You've got the plasma rifle, man. No problem, I'm just a station supervisor."

"Excellent, human," P'Thok looked at the desk. "Harry Dendles," he looked at his men. "Untie the human, he has promised to behave."

His two men nodded excitedly. Of course the human had agreed, he must have recognized P'Thok, Hero of Ice Cream. They untied the human, who sat in his chair, rubbing his arms.

"You aren't going to blow up the station, are you?" Harry asked. P'Thok could smell fear and anxiety pouring off the human and had to resist the urge to shoot the human before it could attack him.

P'Thok shook his head, another thing he had learned on Terra. "No. That would run counter to my purpose and my mission."

"Oh," Harry said. He sighed and pointed at a rectangular package on his desk. "Look, my nerves are shot. Do you mind if I smoke?"

The two warriors looked at P'Thok. Why would the human

be asking if he could emit smoke or maybe even smoulder.

P'Thok remembered cigarettes, dimly, from his time on Terra. It was something humans did when stressed and trying to maintain their emotional comfort or attempting to relax. He nodded. "Of course."

Harry tapped the pack on the desk then opened it, pulling out one. He lit it with a lighter and looked at the big Treana'ad who had its face plate open. He held out the pack. "Want one?"

P'Thok felt a surge of panic as he realized the two other warriors were staring at him. He tried to show no trace of the anxiety he could feel surging up and smell in his own pheromones as he nodded and reached out. He took one, put it in his mandibles, and then accepted a light. He inhaled the smoke and waited to die.

Instead, when he exhaled, the smell of anxiety in his armor faded away, replaced by the soothing smell of the 'smoke'. Standing up straighter, he took another long puff on it, exhaling some out of his mouth.

The smoke rushed down his secondary breathing system, into his big lungs in his abdomen, and filled his blood and ichor system with nicotine. He exhaled through his legs and some out of his mouth, feeling himself calm.

"Do you have another package of smokes?" P'Thok asked mildly. "And a lighting device?"

"Um, sure?" Harry said. He dug an extra pack and lighter out of his desk and handed it to the big insect.

P'Thok's mind felt much clearer, much calmer, as he stood in the station commander's office. He could no longer smell the Terran's fear and anxiety, which made him calmer.

His men stared in shock. They knew P'Thok was a legend, but the fact he was standing there, a lit tube of some kind of plant wrapped in cellulose paper in his mouth, inhaling the smoke, and *not dying* was incredible.

They felt awed in being in his presence.

"What do you need?" Harry asked, realizing he might be able to get out of this with his skin intact. Not only that, he might even be able to convince the Treana'ad not to blow up the station and kill all fifty personnel aboard it.

"When is the next Mantid transport due in?" P'Thok asked, exhaling smoke. His armor was whining a bit about having to push the smoke out of the leg atmospheric ejectors since it ID'd the smoke as an environmental hazard, but he overrode the armor to no longer produce an alarm and to use the ejectors around his footpads.

"I'll have to check the records," Harry said. To be honest, the big Treana'ad warrior, with smoke wafting out around his feet from the cigarette, was a little intimidating. He didn't fidget like the other two, he held perfectly still, staring at him with his compound eyes from inside his helmet.

"No tricks, human Harry Dendles," P'Thok warned, emulating removing the 'smoke' from his mouth and tapping the ashes into the small tray on the human's desk. To be honest, P'Thok was enjoying not having the mission jitters.

Harry just nodded, bringing up the data on his terminal and turning the screen so the big warrior could see it. "Later today."

"Excellent," P'Thok said. "I will be leaving men to guard the station. Once we accomplish our mission we will leave," P'Thok felt a moment of confidence come over him. "Cooperate with me and I will even leave without blowing up your station, sparing all of your lives."

Harry nodded.

"I want you to run a search of your stores. I wish to know if you are in possession of this substance," P'Thok said. He leaned forward and used one bladearm to tap out what he wanted.

Harry checked. They had plenty. It was easy to make and it improved morale. "Yes, we have plenty."

P'Thok nodded. He took another drag and realized he was getting close to the brown end. He tapped one entry on the screen. "Have a container of that brought to the docking bay along with proper implements and some of..." P'Thok leaned closer. "That. Bring a bottle of that."

"Um, of course," Harry said. "I'll have a robot do it. No

tricks."

"Do not hurt the human, just guard him," P'Thok ordered, stubbing out the 'smoke' like the human did. He closed his faceplate. "I will be speaking to the Matron."

The others signalled assent, still amazed at how calm P'Thok had been while dealing with the Terran, who still looked fearsome to them.

P'Thok moved through the station, arriving as the rest of the strike force boarded the station. He ordered them to ensure the humans could not interfere with the mission, but otherwise not to impede them in their tasks.

In the docking bay a robot was waiting and he ordered it to follow him.

He started to feel anxious as he moved through the ship, heading for the Matron's quarters. The pheromones didn't help so he opened his face plate and lite another 'smoke' from the pack. By the second drag he didn't feel as anxious and breathed a long inhalation and exhalation of relief. He tapped a control and his helmet folded up around his neck.

It was not permitted to enter the chambers of a matron with one's head shielded and armored.

He touched the signal pad and waited. The door opened up and immediately the rich thick smell of Matron pheromones filled his senses.

And withdrew when he took a drag off the smoke.

The Matron eyed P'Thok as the large male warrior entered. The sight of him, and his delicious looking head, made her quiver. Once the mission was over, she fully intended upon mating with him and eating his head. She let the pheromones of excitement flow from her, knowing that it would transmit to the big warrior caste Treana'ad.

Instead, he just stood there, some kind of white tube with a beige end in his mouth, the far end burning and wafting a thin stream of smoke.

"Your mission?" The Matron asked, puffing out more pheromones.

P'THOK CHRONICLES

"Part One is complete, oh Matron," P'Thok said, feeling smugness deep inside. Her pheromones were easy to ignore! The smoke leaking out of his collar and wafting up from the burning end masking the pheromones.

The Matron stared at P'Thok, sensing nothing but a deep calm form the warrior.

Perhaps the other Matrons are right. Perhaps there is something special about this one, she mused. *After all, he planned this raid, promised us something we could never dream of.*

P'Thok was keenly aware of the Matron's inspection of him but didn't feel the fear that most males felt in the presence of a Matron. He wasn't afraid that she would suddenly eat his head, and knew that if she moved toward him, he would calmly refuse and run away like any sensible male.

"What is that robot holding?" the Matron asked.

"Proof that what I claim is true," P'Thok said. He turned to the robot, opening the container. He filled a bowl, added some sauce, and put a spoon in it. "Do not eat the bowl or the metal eating implement. Just the soft stuff. Go slowly, it can cause pain if eaten too fast."

He handed the bowl to the Matron, who looked at the small amount in the bottom. "*This* is the miraculous substance you promise will change everything?"

P'Thok nodded. "Yes, Matron."

"Hmm, you better be right," the Matron said. She picked up the metal eating implement, noting that it was freezing cold.

She took a single bite.

It was cold, but tasted amazing. Tastes blossomed in her mouth, when she exhaled through her mouth to warm it the complex protein chains were sensed by her delicate antenna, bringing more pleasure coursing through her mind.

P'Thok smelled the pheromones and quickly lit another cigarette, so he had two in his mouth.

The Matron heeded P'Thok's advice, looking at the male out of the corner of her eye. He was much more handsome than she had previously realized. Virile too. She could tell in the fearless way he looked at her, admiring her beauty. After all, what wasn't to admire. She was a powerful and wise Matron, who had laid many broods of eggs and eaten a hundred heads.

The bowl was empty too quickly and the Matron held out the bowl. "More?" she asked coyly, fluttering her wings, knowing they were flushed with blood.

"More will make you intoxicated to the point of delusions of grandeur," P'Thok warned. "The humans call it 'being high' and it should be avoided."

"Oh," the Matron said, pouting slightly with a droop of the antenna and a sad clacking of her mandibles.

She realized something with a start.

While she definitely hoped that such a fine specimen as P'Thok would realize just how attractive she was, even for an older Matron who's carapace color was beginning to fade, she no longer felt the driving urge to mate. No longer felt the hunger to mate and devour his head. The idea of mating was more a dreamy, drowsy thing that made her abdomen warm rather than a burning desire she couldn't wipe out of her mind.

She looked at the bowl.

"This substance..." she said softly, rubbing her wings together and luxuriating in the drowsy sensual pleasure of it. "This substance is amazing. You were right, we must seize more of it, show it to the Hive Queens, the High Matrons."

P'Thok tapped out a smoke. "Try this, Matron. Another human secret I wrested from them with guile and cleverness."

The arousal and excitement pheromones were thick and the Matron was amazed that P'Thok dared to lean close, put the tube in her mouth, in her sharp and deadly mandibles, and then light the tube.

She inhaled and then exhaled like he suggested.

She felt a calm come over her and the smell of her pheromones receded. Her antenna raised in surprised.

"I will assign one of my men to you, Matron," P'Thok said. "I know they will be safe with you now."

The Matron nodded. To be honest, she'd rather have another little scoop of that wonderful substance and another 'smoke' than eat a male's head.

At least there wasn't a body to dispose of or bury for the grubs to eat when they hatched.

As for himself, P'Thok searched out the stores and found whole cartons of packs of smokes, even little machines that could have liquid added for the same effects. He ordered his men to carry a pack at all times, to have a lit one in their mandibles when approaching the Matron. He took one of the machines and convinced a human to decorate it with precious stones.

The Matron looked up as P'Thok entered her chamber again. She felt a little silly about how she had tried to seduce the big warrior before the mission was over and hoped he would not berate her. Instead, he just knelt down and held a small device and a bottle infuser out to her.

"What is it?" she asked.

P'Thok realized he had no idea what to call it. He thought fast. "A power smoker. Fit only for the wealthy and sophisticated such as yourself, oh Matron."

whew, he thought to himself when he saw her antenna perk up.

She took it and examined it. "What does it do?"

"You simply put the tube in your mouth, press the button, and inhale as if you are using a smoke. I have it loaded with something called 'bubble-gum treat' flavored smoke," P'Thok said, his own basic smoke keeping away the slight tang of misery pheromones.

The Matron followed P'Thok's instructions. She felt a sudden relief as the slight nagging feeling of being a failure left her and her own pheromones receded. The taste was absolutely delicious. She started to take another hit off it and looked at P'Thok.

"May I take more than one 'hit' off of it?" the Matron asked.

"The human who showed me how to use the device, on pain of death," P'Thok lied about that part, "Showed that you can inhale more and completely surround yourself with a thick cloud."

The Matron inhaled deeply, exhaling through her legs as

hard as she could.

The entire room filled with a cloud of vape smoke. It banished old lingering pheromones, wiped away scents of thoughts and discussions before.

The Matron rubbed her wings in shock. "The humans have been keeping this from us?"

"Yes, oh Matron," P'Thok said, exhaling his own smoke. The Matron approved of that. It let her senses know he was there, unlike pheromone maskers, but it was easier to handle.

"Then I hereby approve of your dangerous raid into human space," she said. Her wings quivered slightly. "First, they dare think they can wrest those valuable planets from us, deny us the cold warmth of the red sun and the soft feel of sand and the sweet smell of nitrogen, then they withhold *two* wondrous secrets?"

P'Thok nodded.

"I see more clearly than I have my entire life, P'Thok," the Matron said. "You were right. We must wrest this from the humans. We will commit this raid, show the humans that the Treana'ad are to be taken most seriously," she paused for a moment. "Then we will make our demands to them."

P'Thok nodded slowly and the Matron approved of how solemn the human gesture looked.

"We will demand they cede control of the planets we desire, and give us the secrets of ice cream and smoke," the Matron commanded.

"As you will, oh Matron," P'Thok said. He saluted and began to leave.

"Oh, P'Thok," the Matron called out.

P'Thok slowly turned, feeling fear but the smoke preventing the pheromones from being scented. "Yes, oh Matron?"

"If your raid is successful, you and I shall breed," the Matron said.

P'Thok wanted to scream and run away. He knew it would happen sooner or later. He was doomed!

"What kind was the third variant taste I tried with that sauce?" the Matron asked.

P'THOK CHRONICLES

"Strawberry ripple with hard chocolate shell sauce," P'Thok said.

"Mmm," the Matron hummed, rubbing her wings in please. "Bring that. It tastes better than your head ever could and the shell was pleasantly crunchy. And more of this liquid for my power smoker."

"As you wish, Matron," P'Thok said. He saw the Matron ignoring him, preferring to stare at the star chart. He hurried out, sagging slightly in relief as he walked down the hallway.

His men saw his relaxed saunter and knew that if P'Thok was that sure of the plan, there was no way it could fail.

Soon they would raid the Terrans and the secret of Ice Cream would be theirs!

As for himself, P'Thok raided the store rooms and made sure he took half of the power-smoker liquid.

After all, when a Matron has expressed interest in you, it never hurt to make preparations.

When the Mantid trader docked, their airlock cycled to open up to the umbilical and the Mantid crewmen stared in shock.

A huge Treana'ad warrior stood in the airlock, a cigarette in his mandbles and a plasma rifle in his hand.

"I believe you have my property," P'Thok drawled out, just like the Terran in his favorite Tri-Vee show. He exhaled smoke and motioned with his plasma rifle. "If you comply, you will come to no harm."

The Speaker aboard the vessel weighed the chances. A cigarette smoking Treana'ad with a plasma rifle with at least a full military squad behind him could easily kill his entire crew. The Speaker cursed himself for not bringing a few warriors with him, but all of the warriors were being held back at the Hive Homes.

With a sigh the Speaker gave over command of his ship.

The Treana'ad warriors were unusually focused to the Speaker's psychic senses. The Matron was not the barely repressed ball of breeding urgency, but rather calm and focused on something.

It was strange.

And the Speaker didn't like strange.

He let the usually focused Treana'ad take his ship, trusting in their promises to return soon.

He watched as the ship vanished into jumpspace. He thought, for a second, about overwhelming the minds on the station and taking the Treana'ad ship, but changed his mind. Revealing his abilities now would ruins decades of planning.

Delmek-4 was a standard agricultural planet. They produced wheat, sorghum, corn, soybeans, alfalfa, potatoes, and tobacco. There were sheep, pig, cow, and other animal farms. Factories took the raw food and turned it to foodstuffs, from bread to steaks to mutton to ice cream to cigarettes. True, it was near the Treana'ad Disputed Zone, but it wasn't exactly a priority military target and the close proximity of Mestacalla and the Republic Navy base there at only 7 light years made sure they could scream for help.

P'Thok stood on the bridge, a cigarette in his mandibles, surrounded by the smell of bubble gum as the Matron stared at the planet below.

"You're sure this is the planet we want?" she asked, puffing on her power smoker.

"Positive," P'Thok said confidently. He pointed at the two flattened container labels.

DELMEK ICE CREAM AND DAIRY CORPORATION was written on one.

MANUFACTURED ON DELMEK was on the other.

P'Thok removed the smoke from his mandibles and gestured with it to the pilot. "Take us in for a landing and get ready."

The Matron rubbed her wings together with glee.

And exhaled pink bubblegum vape across the bridge.

She had completely forgotten the burning, all consuming desire to breed.

"The secret of Ice Cream and Cigarettes will be ours!" she crowed.

P'Thok left the bridge, smoke in his mandibles, to gather his men.

A daring raid was waiting.

P'Thok and the Great Ice Cream Raid

Delmek-4 was a standard agricultural planet. They produced wheat, sorghum, corn, soybeans, alfalfa, potatoes, and tobacco. There were sheep, pig, cow, and other animal farms. Factories took the raw food and turned it to foodstuffs, from bread to steaks to mutton to ice cream to cigarettes. True, it was near the Treana'ad Disputed Zone, but it wasn't exactly a priority military target and the close proximity of Mestacalla and the Republic Navy base there at only 7 light years made sure they could scream for help. The Republic shipped the goods of Delmek-4 all over the Republic, supporting the colonies of Terra.

P'Thok was more than a little nervous. Terra Sol was only thirty light years away, the Disputed Zone and Treana'ad Space only ten light years behind him. While Terran Space wasn't big, only roughly 50 light years, and they had possessed nearly fifteen colonies in addition to their heavily protected Core World, P'Thok was still very nervous. He did not mind admitting it to himself, although he found that contemplating it over a bowl of ice cream topped with butterscotch sauce and then smoking a cigarette made it easier to think about.

The Terrans had attempted to colonize two worlds that the Hive Worlds had slated for being used for expansion. Both worlds had been prepared, with the proper creatures in the sand to give grubs a good meal as they grew and the proper vegetation. The Treana'ad couldn't believe the temerity of the Terrans and so they had declared war.

They had even managed to wrest two star systems, both of them with red suns, from the Terrans, and even take two colonies on disgustingly wet worlds underneath dangerous yellow suns.

But unlike every other mammalian race the Treana'ad had discovered, the Terrans could fight. They could fight, and fight hard. Even Mantid warriors and speakers were not as dangerous as a Terran, as the Treana'ad had learned during the two years of warfare.

Which is why P'Thok carefully studied the maps of the primary target that the ship's scanners were able to discern. P'Thok had to admit, the Mantid vessel had *amazing* scanners. He had not expected a Mantid trading vessel to have scanners able to read the dataplate on the back of a ground car from orbit, but he was glad the ship possessed them all the same.

The Matron had agreed, this mission was of great importance. She approved of P'Thok's targets.

The Goody Scoop Ice Cream Company for one. That was the primary target.

The Whachagotta Lose Tobacco Company was the newest target.

P'Thok managed to identify a distribution point for both companies, where trucks full of product came in and were unloaded before the contents were loaded onto a ship to distribute the product around the Republic.

Finally ready, P'Thok entered the bridge and gave the signal.

The pilot, a talented worker caste male who was a good shot with a plasma rifle in addition to being a gifted pilot, glanced at the worker caste at the communications computer, who nodded, a cigarette held in his mandibles.

The communications specialist opened a channel to ground-side.

Right as it was answered the pilot looked at P'Thok.

"Sir, your cigarette," he said.

"Oh," P'Thok took the cigarette out of his mouth and handed it to the pilot.

The screen cleared, showing a beige skinned human with dark hair. "Thontaire City Space Traffic Control. How can I help you?"

"Yes, we need landing permission. We are here to discuss trading with the Mantid Hive Worlds," P'Thok said.

On the side of the screen the overlay of a Mantid Speaker

repeated what P'Thok said, using Mantid body language instead of Treana'ad.

It was an excellent piece of software.

"Berth-9," the human said and cut the channel.

"Well, that was rude," the Matron said, puffing out a cloud of 'blueberry cream' around herself, easing everyone's agitation.

"No matter. I will wrest the ice cream and smoke from them despite their rudeness," P'Thok promised. He looked at the pilot. "Take us in, Klikatikit."

"As you command, sir," the pilot said. He motioned at the cigarette in his mouth. "Do you wish this returned, great one?"

"Keep it. Piloting this ship must be stressful. I for one am grateful for your skills," P'Thok said. He headed for the lift. "I'll be with my men."

The Matron eyes P'Thok as he entered the elevator.

Yes, he would father many grubs.

The Mantid tradeship landed in the dark of night. Two security drones moved close, just in case there was a problem.

Two accurate shots from a heavy plasma rifle gutted them and the two teams of Treana'ad warriors bolted for the two different warehouses while a third sprinted at nearly fifty miles an hour at the spaceport control center.

P'Thok fired his plasma rifle twice, caving in the doors, and rushed in. There was a sign proclaiming which way to security and he waved two men that way. "Stun only!" he reminded them. The other five men followed him as he charged down the hallway, shooting open the door to the control room.

He had carefully examined human media to make sure anything he had to say to humans would carry the most weight. He'd chosen to go without a helmet, instead wearing a cloth head covering like a Terran engaged in nerfarious deeds would, as well as a snazzy hat.

He charged into the room, seeing a half dozen Terran females and a dozen Terran males sitting at work stations.

"REACH FOR THE SKY!" P'Thok yelled out, firing two shots

into the ceiling. "THIS HERE'S A HOLD UP!"

The Terrans stared at the six Treana'ad warriors, easily almost ten feet tall, all of them wearing baclavas and cowboy hats as well as Treana'ad combat armor and carrying Treana'ad plasma rifles.

The raised their hands.

"Keep your fingers off the silent alarms. No cops!" One Treana'ad, excited over it all, ordered, waving his plasma rifle around with one hand and clacking his bladearms together.

"I see a cop, all of you are dead!" another Treana'ad warrior threatened, running over to crouch down and look out the window.

"Nobody do anything stupid and you'll all live to go home to your kids," P'Thok promised, scuttling over to a Terran with the most elaborate decorations, including facial tattoos and piercings. P'Thok pointed at him. "You, Facility Manager, you will do my bidding!"

"I'm the janitor," the impressively decorated human said.

"Oh," P'Thok turned around, reaching into his combat harness. The Terrans flinched. "Who's the manager?"

A Terran human gulped and raised her hand.

P'Thok pulled out his pack of cigarettes, opened it, then lit the one he retrieved.

The humans seemed to relax as P'Thok put the pack away.

"Come over here, stand by me. Anyone pulls anything, I see any cops, and you'll be first," P'Thok threatened.

The terran female nodded, moving over by the massive Treana'ad.

"Smoke?" P'Thok asked. Now that he had them all cowed and submissive, the movies had shown that he should be polite and sociable.

"Um, thank you?" The Terran said. She lit it and handed the pack back.

P'Thok watched two of his men quickly search the desks for passwords, finding them, and then going to work on the computers. One man was to get the robotic system to lay the loading tracks to the ship, the other was to start listing freight to be loaded. A third man crouched down in front of a terminal and began furiously typing, searching the Terran InfoNet for the information that the Treana'ad so desperately needed.

The fourth and fifth crouched down by the windows, peeking out, watching for 'cops'. One opened the window and stuck the barrel of his grenade launcher out, an EM-homing grenade loaded up.

After a moment, P'Thok realized that the room had both male and female Terrans in it, and the Terran next to him was the largest of them. Thick of body and limb.

"You have many males here. Are they all yours?" P'Thok asked.

"Uh, they work for me," the shift manager said, her mind whirling at what was happening.

"No, no, are they yours for when you are overcome by breeding lust?" P'Thok asked. "What of the lesser females?"

"Um, I don't get overcome by breeding lust," the Terran said.

P'Thok turned and looked down at her. "You don't? Does that mean you don't enter breeding heat and... what's that thing mammals do... ovulate! right, don't you ovulate and devour the lesser females and then breed with your males?"

"No. I use birth control," the female said.

"Birth... control?" P'Thok said. He tapped his bladearms nervously against his chest plate. "What is 'birth control'? Tell me, and perhaps I will reward you."

The Terran female just stared. "Um, it's just an implant. It releases hormones into my bloodstream that keeps me from ovulating, releasing eggs into my womb, so I can't get pregnant unless I want to turn off the implant."

P'Thok thought for a long moment. That seemed impossible. Controlling breeding cycles? Why, you might as well try to control pheromone...

...

P'Thok pulled out his small datapad and handed it to the

Terran. "Write down everything you know about this 'birth control' and when we leave I will spare all of your lesser females and captive males."

"Of course. Just... don't hurt them, OK?" the female Terran said.

P'Thok just nodded, his mind spinning. *Controlling egg production? It's crazy. It's insane. It's impossible... but what if it isn't? What if it can be done?*

"Sir! I've got it! They left that part of the database unsecure! There's *hundreds* of recipes!" his warrior searching InfoNet said excitedly.

"Download it all! We are indeed lucky, men," P'Thok said.

"The hold is 90% full, sir," the one watching the robotic loading systems said.

"Sir, we need to know something," the one tagging inventory to be loaded.

"What?" P'Thok asked.

"Where does 'milk' come from?" the warrior asked.

P'Thok turned to the lead female. "Where does milk come from?"

"Cows. Moo-moos," the Terran said. She tapped the notepad. "Those."

P'Thok stared. There were millions of the brown furred four legged herbivores on the planet. Of course! It made perfect sense!

"Stop loading!" P'Thok said. "We need to save room!" he turned to the human. "Input the care and feeding of moomoos."

The shift leader was completely confused as she did it. Complying with hostage takers was the best way to survive a hostage situation, but what they wanted was so confusing. She handed the small datapad back.

"Signal the teams! Withdraw to the ship. We must carry out an additional mission!" P'Thok said.

When the two watching the window counted that all the Treana'ad were aboard the ship, P'Thok busted out the window with the butt of his plasma rifle and had his men climb out. He looked at the Terrans.

"Thank you for your cooperation," he said, then raced off at top speed for the ship.

The Matron watched as P'Thok entered the bridge, exhaling smoke from his legs.

"Find a large grouping of these creatures," P'Thok ordered, tossing the image from his datapad to the main viewscreen. "Set down, quietly, near them. They are easily startled and weigh as much as warrior."

"What are those?" the Matron asked, exhaling blueberry cream, which seemed to calm the bridge crew the best.

"Moomoos. They are the animal that produces the substance known as 'milk', which is mammary gland nutrient fluid. It's the secret ingredient to ice cream!' P'Thok said excitedly, taking another drag off his cigarette.

"Located. Not far away," the pilot said. He looked back. "We're setting down."

"We'll collect some males as well as females," the Matron ordered. "I shall have several old grub hatcheries converted to habitats for them!" she could imagine the envy of all the other Matrons, including the local Hive Queen if she built lavish moomoo habitats to ensure the production of ice cream.

"As you command, Matron," P'Thok said, still thinking over what the human had said. She wasn't consumed by breeding frenzies, she could control her urge to breed and give birth. Treana'ad society, since the dawn of time, had centered all around breeding cycles.

Wars had been fought over breeding grounds.

The majority of males were fated to die at the mandibles of females.

Controlling breeding, as insane as it sounded, as impossible as the concept seemed, could break that cycle that dominated Treana'ad life.

And P'Thok knew he'd really really like to keep his head uneaten, especially with the Matron's spoken desire to mate with him.

P'THOK CHRONICLES

"I must go command my men," P'Thok said. The Matron waved idly, exhaling smoke, as she imagined the incredulous rival Matrons who would gnaw at their own bladearms with envy at the lavish habitats she would construct.

The ship landed with a bump and the rear cargo hatch lowered. The moomoos paid no attention as the Treana'ad warriors rushed out to meet them and stopped.

"Get on the ship," P'Thok ordered, waving his plasma rifle at the moomoo.

The moomoo opened one eye, looked at him, and closed its eye again.

"Sir, the moomoo is ignoring my commands!" one of his men said, rubbing his wings in agitation.

P'Thok stared at the mammal. It was huge, massing maybe even more than a warrior. It was heavy with muscle, a thick furry hide, a large head, and a ring in the nose. It was studiously ignoring him and he realized with surprise that the creature was asleep.

Curious, he reached out and grabbed the ring. It was warm and slightly slimy and the moomoo opened its eyes.

"This way, moomoo, this way," P'Thok chittered, gently tugging the ring.

The moomoo followed.

"Emulate me, men," P'Thok ordered. He led the moomoo onboard the ship, then rushed out to another one. And another. And another.

He sent ten of his men out to grab the large bales of grain, something called alfalfa and yellow ones called 'hay', and then approached one of the even larger ones with horns. He grabbed the ring and said "follow me, moomoo, follow me."

The large moomoo's eyes opened, it glared, and suddenly rushed forward, slamming into P'Thok and knocking him into the air before stopping, passing gas, and going still again. One hoof pawed at the ground for a moment.

"Sir!" one shouted, leveling his plasma rifle.

"No, just stun it! Get a graviton loader, we'll carry it and put it in a stall," P'Thok ordered.

They had nearly all of the moomoos loaded up when P'Thok heard a human shout.

He turned and saw a human with a rifle.

"CATTLE RUSTLERS! BOY, CALL THE SHERIFF!" the human yelled, leveling the rifle and firing. The round whizzed by P'Thok.

"Men, retreat! We must hurry before the Sheriff arrives!" P'Thok called out, imagining a huge warmech with a star painted on its chest like he had seen in the Space Marshall Bravestar documentary videos.

He and his men rushed back onto the ship, one pulling a grav-dolly with an unconscious mean moomoo on it.

The human chased them, waving his rifle and firing shots that kept missing.

Once aboard P'Thok slapped the com button. "Lift off! Hurry! The cops are coming!"

The ship lifted off even as the cargo ramp slowly raised.

P'Thok breathed a sigh of relief as the ship screamed into space, breaking orbit and vanishing into jumpspace. He slumped in relief as he lit a smoke and sought out the Matron.

She was just finishing a small bowl of ice cream, the room full of the scent of bubblegum.

"Matron, our raid is even more successful then we thought," P'Thok said.

"Oh?" The Matron signified interest. She had to admit, P'Thok was quite handsome. She fluttered her wings and gave him a coy look, feeling like a young matron again.

P'Thok checked his notepad. The Terran had put information about 'birth control' on it, including describing it, describing the mechanism by which it worked, and even the different brands and types, many were confusing and obviously intended for mammalian biology.

"Keep an open mind, as you did about ice cream and smoke," P'Thok said. He handed her the notepad. "Another human secret I wrested from them with guile and cunning."

The Matron looked at the data and suddenly stopped. She

exhaled bubblegum scent slowly then took a deep drag off of her power smoker.

"The concept is insane!" she blurted out. "But... but... how did we never think of this? How did we never think of any of this?"

"Would you do it if you could, Matron?" P'Thok asked, tensing to run out of the room if she took offense. "I mean, if you could break the tyranny of the birthing chamber, would you do it?"

The Matron nodded. "Yes. It consumes a Matron's life. This... this seems so impossible, yet so simple. An impossible concept, an easily achieved medical research project."

She sighed wistfully. "To be freed."

"Then accept that notepad, Matron, with my undying awe at your presence," P'Thok said, backing out of the room.

The Matron didn't even notice, puffing absently on her power smoker and reading the articles downloaded from the Terran InfoNet and the testimony of a Terran Shift Leader, an obviously important and grand station.

To be free... she thought as the ship raced for the space station.

P'Thok Makes a Video

The three videos hit InfoNet like atomic bombs.

They were each viewed in the billions of times in the first 72 hours. Then watched and rewatched over and over.

Each video spawned hundreds, thousands of imitators seeking to prove or disprove the videos, all of them doing nothing more than proving they existed. On all eight planets the videos were played even on the public access Tri-Vee channels. Even children watched them.

The first two were very much alike.

"Smoking for the Survival Oriented Male" was the first one. It showed a Treana'ad warrior caste with a nifty looking hat putting a white tube with one brown end in his mouth and lighting the opposite end, with a warning to always ensure the brown end was held in the mandibles. How to get a good drag off of it, and how to force the smoke out of the spiracles in the legs. The video showed how to stop arguments by lighting a cigarette, how to defuse tension, how to even approach a Matron or matron and ask for directions to the nearest public entertainment facility.

The viewers were amazed at how confident the male was. Some attempted to attribute it to his marvelous hat, after all, it made him look dangerous and competent and rugged. Still others were concerned that without the hat the 'smoke' wouldn't work.

The "Moomoo Carer Hat Corporation" went from little more than an InfoNet Store to being worth trillions in the space of a week as they were swamped with orders. Every male wanted one, from the lowest street sweeper to the semi-captive breeding male of a powerful High Matron who hoped the hat would help him escape his eventual fate.

The second video, titled "Power Smoking for the Elegant Matron" featured an obviously wealthy and powerful Matron, resplendent in jewelry, an animal leather vest, a decorated sash, and her antenna adorned with star shaped charms, using a device to inhale sharply then exhale huge clouds of smoke from her spiracles. It showed how she could stop arguments, prevent recently matured, just molted females from overwhelming a male with pheromones, ease discomfort of those who had fought the Terrans and survived, and even calm the highly aggressive hatchlings.

The video was watched over and over.

The "Designer Power Smoker" corporation and the "Senso-Taste Smoke Juice" corporation were flooded with orders to the point where powerful High Matrons petitioned their local Hive Queens to move them up on the order list, since both corporations were militantly "first come first serve" when it came to filling orders.

The Hive Queens all sipped at their ornate and sparkly power-smokers, listened to the complaints of the High Matrons, and universally (as agreed during the meetings) used "Sour Apple Surprise" to signal their displeasure and ordered the High Matrons to return to their lavish estates and be grateful that the world was changing.

Which startled the High Matrons, as they knew that either they would have their request granted or be eaten by the Hive Queen's grubs.

The Hive Queens of all eight worlds *knew* that the next one would change Treana'ad destiny even more than the (totally on purpose and not at all accidental) discovery of jumpspace and jumpspace superluminal flight. They had argued, worried, considered, and debated the release of the third video.

But they agreed, like the (totally on purpose and not at all accidental) invention of the jump-drive had, that to try to stand in the way of the destiny of the Treana'ad was a good way to get run over and left like a flying insect on a groundcar's windscreen.

So the video hit InfoNet.

And promptly crashed the servers.

The beginning of the video was... controversial to say the least.

Four just molted young adult females were arguing in a room, each having taken up a corner, chittering angrily at one another, sharpening bladearms, hurling insults, their wings and carapaces flush with blood and shining brightly.

A matron entered with a power smoker and exhaled a huge cloud of smoke that filled the room and rolled over the young females. They calmed, no longer throwing insults, but the anger was still almost palpable even over the video. The matron produced four bowls, handing one to each of the females. Each bowl contained two small roundish orbs of something creamy looking that glittered with frost. The females ate the orbs and seemed to get drowsy, quickly moving to embrace one another and reaffirm their familial bonds and friendship.

Everyone who saw the video knew that what they had seen was impossible. The four females should have engaged in an orgy of slaughter until only one was left, and statistically, there was a high chance that all four would have died.

The next part started out confusing. A Matron entered the room with a worker caste, who had on one of the neato hats. The worker was carrying a bowl of ice in one hand and a bag of stuff in the other. As the viewers watched the worker, under the supervision of the obviously wealthy and powerful Matron, brought out two metal can with plas lids. The two cans were empty, which the worker showed off. First the worker put ice in the bottom of the larger can, then mixed ingredients in the smaller. Something called "Moomoo Juice" and other esoteric ingredients. Not many, really, just four that were listed as "IMPORTANT". The kilikik fruit that was chopped into small chunks was listed as optional as was the crushed iktakvak nuts. Once the ingredients were in the smaller can, the worker put the lid on it. Then the worker put ice in the bottom of the big metal can, sprinkled sea salt on it, then placed the small can on top of the ice. Then four layers of ice, each time salt was put on it, then covered the smaller can and put the lid on it. The worker then wrapped the large can in a cloth.

Then was a cut away scene where the worker used his bladearms to roll the can back and forth for a long time. The video advised the male to have a smoke during this time.

When the worker was done, he opened the large can, removed the smaller, then made sure the camera had a good view of him opening the small can.

A wondrous substance was revealed. A thick semi-solid that was extremely cold but still soft. He pulled out a bowl, scooped out two small orbs with a bejeweled scooper (Available in limited quantities for only 350 credits! BUY NOW!) and handed the bowl to the matron. He then repeated it for three other bowls and it became obvious to the viewer that this was the substance given to the recently matured females!

Treana'ad rushed to the nearest store, only to find huge lines waiting. The stores were prepared and had hired matrons to walk the lines with power smokers, exhaling sweet smoke, to keep the Treana'ad in the lines calm. It was limited to two bags of ingredients per person, but the stores sold out in hours.

The Hive Queens had foreseen this, however, and had hovertrucks waiting to restock the stores while matrons dressed in Hive Security Armor wandered the lines with power smokers to keep everyone calm.

If the first three videos were atomic bombs, the fourth was a planet cracker.

Reserved for mature audiences only, it showed a Matron mating with a warrior caste male. Every matron who viewed it nodded along. A powerful and obviously fit male. He would sire excellent grubs, and his head would undoubtedly be delicious, causing the matron to release powerful hormones that would ensure healthy and strong grubs.

The males had seen videos like this before.

They knew how it ended.

Instead, she ate a scoop of the 'ice cream', then took a deep drag from her power smoker, and *then* mated. While matind she used her bladearms to slice curls of ice cream from the second orb. When the mating was done, she rapidly ate the third, took a hit from her power smoker, and ordered the male from her presence. It ended with "ICE CREAM AND SMOKE SAVES LIVES!"

He had escaped!

The males cheered for the escaped doomed male.

The females rewound the video and watched it again.

The Treana'ad numbered in the high tens of billions across their eight planets. There were thousands, tens of thousands who needed to breed.

Nearly 15% of them tried the method in the video. Almost of a third of those recording what occurred.

To the shock of everyone, the males survived, escaping while the matron relaxed, puffing on her power smoker and nibbling at the residual tastes on the tips of her bladearms.

Traditionalists wanted the videos banned, citing irreversible damage to society and the way things had always been.

The Male Resistance fractured as one half wanted the videos banned, knowing that political power would slip from their graspers, the other half seeing the videos as proof that no longer would males be destined to die just so that the Treana'ad people could endure.

The Hive Queens of the eight planets, forty-nine in all, eight of whom (one on each world) had bred with a war hero who had survived what would have been a fatal meeting, demanded the videos stayed up.

And what the Hive Queens wanted, the Treana'ad people acquiesced to.

Those four videos hit the Treana'ad species like a runaway train into a moomoo.

The Hive Queens demanded Moomoo Raids into Terran Space. If the Terrans would not share the Moomoos, then the Hive Queens would take the Moomoos.

The Matron who had financed and approved the daring night time raid that had wrested the secrets of ice cream and smoke and even snatched moomoos, who had been promoted to a High Matron, had a different suggestion.

She proposed another daring plot.

She would take a ship into Terran Space, with the War Hero to accompany her along with his faithful and dauntless combat team, and demand that the Terrans send a diplomat to speak with her. She would demand that the Terrans turn over the two red star systems to the Treana'ad people, open trade relations to the Treana'ad People, and in the Treana'ad People's benevolence, they'd return the worthless rainy and plant covered planets around those dangerous yellow stars.

The Hive Queens discussed the plan. It was insane, impossible.

Then the newly crowned High Matron reminded them that the concept of 'birth control' had also seemed impossible, but it had taken Treana'ad scientists less than a *month* to create a synthetic hormone that prevented breeding hysteria.

The Queens ate ice cream, puffed on their power smokers, and consulted one another.

If it didn't work, then all the Treana'ad people lost was one ship, a newly promoted High Matron, and a war hero who had already bred an outlandish and impossible ten times.

They made the decision.

"Peace or Bust" was commissioned and went into jump-space, heading for the Terran/Treana'ad Disputed Zone.

Admiral John Tshuma rushed into the bridge of the flagship of the *Enterprise*, still buttoning his tunic as the red lights flashed and the klaxon wailed.

"What have got?" he asked, rubbing his face. His jaw ached from the nosleep inhaler he'd puffed on in the elevator.

"Treana'ad ship. Just one. Looks unarmed. It jumped in at the resonance zone and started broadcasting," LT JG Duong said. "They're sitting right next to a hypercom buoy and are waiting to talk."

That was new. Treana'ad usually showed up with hive ships, dropping tens of thousands of warriors onto a planet and spawning thousands of torch-ship fighters. Just one ship, asking to talk, was something that had never happened since the Treana'ad had attacked out of the blue.

"All right, is our hypercom link warmed up?" Tshuma asked.

The LT nodded and the bridge crew tensed.

"Open the link," Tshuma ordered. The screen cleared of the

Republic's wallpaper, the image of the Treana'ad appearing.

Tshuma coughed, avoiding bursting out laughing. There was a huge one, possibly a female, with cloth draped over her(?) abdomen, wearing a leather vest with a silver star on the breast, and a sash covered with ornaments as well as a dangling star from the end of each of her antenna.

The male warriors were what was worse. All but the center one were wearing balaclavas, with imitation Stetson cowboy hats, leather vests with brass stars over body armor, with crossed leather belts packing plasma pistols. The male, an obvious warrior caste, in the center of the picture was not wearing a balaclava, but instead had a cigarette in his mouth.

"This is Admiral John Tshuma, of the Republic Naval Vessel *Enterprise*," he said. "Whom am I speaking with?"

"I am P'Thok, and my words are backed by ice cream and cigarettes so you will heed to the demands of the Treana'ad People!"

P'Thok Signs His Name

The High Matron exhaled Blue Raz Cotton Candy in a thick cloud, dispelling the anxious feel of the room as she entered. She looked at her gathered assistants, which consisted of P'Thok's combat team, two Matrons, and six Young Matrons. She folded her bladearms under her sash and gave out a pleased hum before rubbing her wings together for a moment.

"P'Thok?" she said mildly, taking a small sip off of her power-smoker.

"Yes, Matron?" the big warrior caste Treana'ad answered.

"How close have you been to Terrans without combat?" she asked.

"When I was on Terra I bumped them quite often. They usually did not take offense," P'Thok said.

"Have you interacted with them much?" the Matron asked.

"Only while interrogating them subtly with my spy training," P'Thok said, watching the lights on the wall change from red to yellow, signalling that the docking tube had locked on.

"Are they truthful or deceitful?" she asked.

"Both. They deceive not only others but themselves," P'Thok answered. "However, for the most part, you can rely on them to do as they have promised."

"Good, good," the Matron said. "I know they are fierce combatants, unusually strong and aggressive for primates, with intelligence to match typical primate cleverness. I was just wondering if we could believe any promises they make to the Treana'ad people."

P'Thok thought for a long moment about what he had seen on Terra. A confusing welter of memories behind ice cream overdose and fear.

"I believe so," P'Thok said. "They can be impulsive and rash, they have no real concept of personal danger, but unlike the Mantid and much like us they are individuals, not a hive mind."

"Good, good," the Matron stepped backwards slightly as the

airlock irised open.

P'Thok led the group down the armored docking corridor, keeping his hands away from the two plasma pistols he had in holsters. He had gotten used to wearing the weapons in such a manner as he had assisted the Matron in convincing the Hive Queens the value of his discoveries. Moomoos didn't like the big rifles, it made the mean moomoos aggressive to carry a rifle, but the pistols they ignored.

At the far end was a human delegation. Armored Terrans with sidearms in holsters on their belts, matte black cybernetic arms, eyes that glowed a soft amber color that P'Thok found comfortable. He was larger than the Terrans but knew that one on one they were the better fighters. There were six Terrans in uniforms with braids and jeweled ribbons in a stack as well as fancy hats with wide polished brims.

He didn't let it worry him, he wasn't here to fight.

"How should I address you?" the uniformed Terran with the fanciest hat and the most braids and jeweled ribbons asked, stepping forward.

P'Thok held up one hand, turning the High Matron. "He wishes to know how he should address you."

"High Matron Me'Luki will suffice, as the Hive Queens renamed me," the High Matron said.

P'Thok turned back to the Terran with the fanciest hat, idly wondering how he would look in it and if it would be appealing to females within reason. "You may address her as High Matron Me'Luki."

The Terran gave a stiff formal nod that P'Thok had learned from his time on Terra was a gesture of assent and agreement.

"If the High Matron Me'Luki will accompany us, we can move straight to the diplomatic suite, unless she would prefer to delay," the fancy one said. His body language showed no deceit or ill-will toward the High Matron or P'Thok from what the insectiod warrior had learned from his spy mission about Terran body language.

P'Thok repeated it, making sure to include a translation for the subtle movements of the primate's face and body.

"They do not use pheromones, High Matron, so much of their conversations take place by expressions on their faces as well as how they move their bodies," P'Thok told her.

"How interesting," the High Matron mused, staring at the hat on the fanciest dressed one's head. It radiated authority and command and she found it fascinating with all the polished gold braid.

She decided that she would demand it as part of the peace process and have P'Thok wear it for their next breeding. The High Matron felt that the large warrior would look particularly dashing and dominating in such a fine headgear.

The Terrans led them deep into the small but deadly Terran battleship. They needed much less space than the Treana'ad for corridors and maintenance spaces as well as crew stations and P'Thok could tell they had devoted it to additional armor, weapon systems, and defensive measures.

The ship vibrated sheer menace and promise of lethality around the Treana'ad and one by one they all lit cigarettes at the High Matron's command.

The admiral wondered for a moment if he should let the Treana'ad diplomatic mission know that smoking was prohibited on Republic military vessels, then changed his mind when he realized they had all been getting agitated before the big High Matron had chittered something at them and they lit their cigarettes.

With my luck it'd be some kind of terrible cultural snafu to make them stop smoking, the admiral thought to himself.

He led the High Matron and her accompaniment, all wearing balaclavas and cowboy hats, to the briefing room. It had been cleared out and then had additional recording and surveillance systems added in to make sure that every detail was recorded of the first meeting between Treana'ad and Human that wasn't over gunsights.

The High Matron appraised the room before stepping into it. Her delicate antenna could detect the electromagnetic frequencies in the air and she highly approved of the vast array of recording devices that were undoubtedly there to record her magnificent presence. She noted the table was an oval and she motioned for the other females to stand against the wall, each guarded by two warriors, and moved to one end, P'Thok next to her.

The Admiral noted what she did and signalled his own staff to line the opposite walls, sitting down with the JAG lawyer beside him.

"Now, High Matron Me'Luki, are you willing to inform the Terran Republic what this is all about?" the Admiral asked, staring at the High Matron but knowing the big warrior, the only one not wearing a balaclava, would do all the talking.

"The Treana'ad People wish to present their demands upon the Terran Republic. Meet these demands, if you are willing, and there will be peace between our peoples," P'Thok translated the High Matron's words.

The Terran just nodded and P'Thok noted that his face went still, the micro-expression disappearing, and that his escort all went perfectly still.

"Very well, please table your demands," the Admiral said.

The High Matron frowned, then leaned forward, speaking directly into the table's surface.

"Table! Heed my words, for they are backed with ice cream and cigarettes! As is the will of the Hive Queens, you will return to us the two systems you have taken, open up trade of moomoos, ice cream, and cigarettes, and we will return your two yellow star systems. Accomplish this, and there will be peace between us," the High Matron said.

The table dutifully printed out her statement in Treana'ad script and the strange blocky Terran script that looked so artless and crude.

The High Matron remembered what she had decided and looked up at the Terran even as she continued to speak. "And I demand your leader's fancy head ornamental covering."

"Um, she doesn't actually have to speak *at* the table. It's a phrase that means present your demands," the Terran Admiral said.

The High Matron glanced at the females and saw the agitation at what they felt was a calculated humiliation toward her by the Terran Admiral. She took a hit from her power smoker and exhaled a cloud of Carnival Cotton Candy Bliss around herself.

The Admiral, who had been able to smell the sharp acrid smell of agitated Treana'ad and could see the movements of the brightly colored (what he assumed was) females, was startled to see them all calm down immediately when the largest one took a hit from her vape and then exhaled a cloud that filled the room.

It dawned on him immediately what he had just seen. He reached down and overrode the environmental system before it would start working on clearing the room of the smoke.

"First clarification, what is a 'moomoo'?" the Admiral asked.

"One of these," P'Thok said, setting down a cube. He ignored the slight shifting of the Terran guards and the way the amber glow in their eyes grew stronger.

He was a warrior. He knew the Terran eyes would go red before they were really dangerous.

A cow appeared over the holocube, happily chewing on a mouthful of cud, surrounded by luxurious grass underneath a massive dome. A bull appeared beside it, pawing its hoof and menacing several worker Treana'ad who were offering it food.

"Both the milk moomoos and the mean moomoos," P'Thok said, "are vital to this agreement."

The Admiral wondered if he'd suddenly gone insane. Sure, it explained the night-time raid three months ago where the Treana'ad had made off with hundreds of head of cattle, not to mention a dozen ice cream trucks and a hold full of ice cream and cigarettes, but...

seriously?

"You wish to open up trade, specifically 'moomoos', cigarettes, and ice cream?" the Admiral asked. "In addition to giving us back the two systems you took?"

"Only if you also agree to return the red giant systems you

took. Those are vital and are not open for discussion," the High Matron said through P'Thok.

P'Thok made sure to moderate the tone and agitation.

"Might I ask why those systems are so vitally important to you?" the Admiral asked.

The High Matron scoffed. "As if you didn't know that those are the only systems where planets that civilized beings prefer. We *know* their value, humans, just as we know those yellow star systems are so dangerous as to be nearly worthless due to the solar activity and harsh radiation."

The Admiral glanced at his JAG Officer.

Did I just have a stroke? he asked the JAG Officer over his datalink.

Not unless I just had one too, the JAG Officer answered.

The Admiral thought fast. The Treana'ad had attacked without warning only a few years prior. He used his datalink to check the two systems that the High Matron was demanding.

One was taken in combat after nearly a year's worth the fighting that had a horrific casualty rate. The Treana'ad kept assaulting the system, kept trying to take it back.

The other had been surveyed and a colony placed on it only ten years ago.

The Admiral looked at the dates.

The Treana'ad had attacked *after* the colony was founded on the sandy cool planet that was stuck in the middle of the Amber Zone. It had a high nitrogen content, very little wind, and was virtually covered with the local equivalent of trees.

The checked the other planet.

Same kind of trees. Exactly.

He had a sudden, sinking feeling.

"The Terran Republic demands that the Terrans present on the first world be returned without harm to the Republic at the Treana'ad People's expense," the Admiral said. "Not held as hostages or slaves."

It took a minute for the High Matron to be informed on the meaning of the last two concepts.

"Of course, the Treana'ad People are a wise and graceful race. Are you sure they would leave such wondrously lush and lavish planets to dwell somewhere else? We can protect them from the Great Hatching," the High Matron said.

Oh... no...

"Ahem, well, perhaps it might be best if they returned to the Republic until our peace can be formalized and our people understand each other better?" the Admiral tried.

The High Matron gave a solemn nod, something she had practiced repeatedly on the trip.

"An excellent point," the Maton said. "Agreed," she turned to P'Thok. "You were correct, P'Thok, they are most agreeable after a scoop of ice cream," she looked back at the Admiral. "I must insist upon your head covering. I covet it greatly."

The treaty took six days to finalize. Both sides felt as if they were getting everything they wanted, especially when the Admiral informed his staff that the Terran Republic had apparently colonized and started to terraform a planet that had already been xenoformed.

The Treana'ad Ambush had not come out of the blue.

It had been in response to the Terran act of war.

The signing was lavish, to the High Matron.

It took place in a landing craft hangar. A wide open space, with the assault shuttles idling at the sides, ranks of Terran Republic Marines drawn up respectfully to witness, and her own envoys at attention. The High Matron, escorted by P'Thok, danced up to the table and signed her name in the delicate formal script, with a pen that left behind gold. She stepped back and motioned at P'Thok.

"None of this would have happened without your genius," she told him. "You shall sign for all males, as I have signed for the Hive Queens."

P'Thok nodded, signing his name with a flourish.

The Admiral presented his extra dress hat to the High Matron.

And the Human/Treana'ad War came to an end.

MANTID FREE WORLDS

Are you watching those old videos again?

---NOTHING FOLLOWS---

TREANA'AD HIVE WORLDS

Yeah. I wanted to show our new siblings.

---NOTHING FOLLOWS---

TELKAN FORGE WORLDS

So, wait, she wanted the hat because she believed it granted some kind of powers?

---NOTHING FOLLOWS---

TREANA'AD HIVE WORLDS

Since she laid a clutch that nearly twenty survived to adulthood, she wasn't wrong.

---NOTHING FOLLOWS---

MANTID FREE WORLDS

That whole war was just so goofy.

---NOTHING FOLLOWS---

AKLTAK FREE FLIGHT FORESTS

Both sides were so new. The Terrans had only claimed those worlds, they hardly had any presence on them and the Treana'ad had less than ten.

---NOTHING FOLLOWS---

TREANA'AD HIVE WORLDS

That's why those two worlds were so important. There was a Great Hatching coming and we desperately needed the room.
It could have been ugly.

---NOTHING FOLLOWS---

TNVARU HOME

How so?

---NOTHING FOLLOWS---

TREANA'AD HIVE WORLDS

Back then, it was a little savage. See, the eggs are laid, then they hatch to grubs. The grubs eat the roots and bugs in the ground and each other. About half the grubs get eaten by their siblings.

Then they make a cocoon and when the cocoon hatches the little hatchling ones come out. Those ones are highly aggressive. The male ones run to the outside while the females begin fighting over territory. About two thirds of the females kill each other. The males began metamorphosing into worker and warrior caste. The warriors fight it out with each other at first, about a third of them die. The workers build fortifications, about twenty percent work themselves to death. Then the females overwhelm several warriors and a couple dozen workers, then take over a fortification. They fight until the end of puberty in little petty wars between fortresses.

A Great Hatching means *a trillion* eggs laid, across a planet.

It's pretty savage. Luckily, a Great Hatching is, *was*, only every couple centuries.

---NOTHING FOLLOWS---

TELKAN FORGE WORLDS

My God. How many of your young in each generation died fighting each other?

---NOTHING FOLLOWS---

TREANA'AD HIVE WORLDS

Before the P'Thok Liberation?

Eighty percent killed and ate each other before adulthood on average.

---NOTHING FOLLOWS---

...

...

...

MANTID FREE WORLDS

"We die free."

---NOTHING FOLLOWS---

TREANA'AD HIVE WORLDS

Exactly.

---NOTHING FOLLOWS---

TNVARU GESTALT THINGY

My God...

---NOTHING FOLLOWS---

HOW P'THOK TOTALLY ON PURPOSE AND NOT AT ALL ACCIDENTALLY SAVED CHRISTMAS

The Terran girl with cat ears, a fuzzy face, whiskers, and a big smile stuck her tongue out at P'Thok, wiggling where her legs met her torso and leaning forward, one hand coming forward to show two fingers in a V shape.

P'Thok clacked his mandibles at his opponent and waited.

The music started, fast paced, quick beat, and his opponent, a hologram, began jumping back and forth on the squares lighting up. P'Thok copied her, his four legs to her two, rapidly moving to hit the squares as soon as they lit up.

The high score on the musical agility tester would be his, oh yes it would.

The other Treana'ad warriors stared in awe as P'Thok jumped up, turned 90 degrees, and landed smoothly, his footpads flashing as he hit each square as soon as it lit up, waving his hands with the holographic guide, matching the overly flexible Terran girl move for move, despite having four legs.

The machine recognized P'Thok's greatness as the crew watched, squeaking out "Perfect!" "Excellent" "Kawaii!" as he moved.

The lights in the exercise room flashed and everyone looked up.

P'Thok ignored it, concentrating on his digital opponent. The agility trainer had been bought from a Terran trader on the planet they had left only days before, heading for the jump point before going to jumpspace to take a load of moomoos and bacca back to Smokey Cone itself.

"Strike Leader P'Thok, report to the bridge," the Captain's voice came over the speakers.

P'Thok ignored it, his footpads stomping down, the agility trainer showering him with holographic sparks, whirling spirals of light, and holographic hearts and streamers.

He was almost finished, the other warrior caste of the Treana'ad Strike Team starting to cheer.

Whatever the Captain wanted took second place to the demanding training of a Treana'ad warrior.

The song ended and P'Thok bent at the waist, flourishing his bladearms to the Terran girl. She jumped up and down, clapping her hands and making the high pitched squeaking of barely mature Terrans.

"HIGH SCORE!" the machine bellowed.

P'Thok turned from girl and flourished his bladearms at his men, who watched in amazement as their leader, the legendary P'Thok, walked off of the platform with a swagger, his abdomen barely pulsating as he breathed heavy.

"Practice hard, men, and you shall find your agility skills serving you well upon Smokey Cone in case the Terrans suddenly attack again!" P'Thok said. He adjusted his moomoo hat and got out a pack of cigarettes as the lights flashed again.

"Strike Leader P'Thok, report to the bridge," the ship Captain repeated again.

P'Thok made sure to saunter, a skill he'd practiced since he'd seen humans do it, all the way to the bridge, puffing on a cigarette as he rubbed his vestigial wings together in pleasure. He had defeated the Terran girl, who was a virtual construct, and proved his superiority to all who had watched.

"High score," he clacked, savoring the words. Terran words, for supremacy over all others who might even view the scores, much less attempt to unseat the holder of the high score.

The lift opened and P'Thok moved out onto the bridge.

The Captain looked at the legendary hero as the big warrior moved into the bridge, his MooMoo Wrangler head covering on, a smoke in his mandibles. He was nervous being in the presence of such a legendary personage, but still, P'Thok was the leader of the strike team as well as the Treana'ad who spoke to humans on the trading planet.

"Yes, Captain?" P'Thok asked, exhaling smoke around his footpads and from his abdomen.

"We detected what appears to be a damaged emergency beacon," the Captain said. "We dropped from jumpspace and this is what appeared on our scanners."

P'Thok turned from the Captain and looked at the screen.

A ship hung in the blackness of space. It was a standard early generation ship. A long cylinder with four fins around the engine and a cone on one end. It was lit up by lines of multicolored lights spiralling around it and the tip of the nosecone was blinking red. The entire thing was colored green and had blinking lights all over it. Additionally, it had two arcs of metal, with spines sticking off into the arc, that were old oxidized endosteel.

"It does not fit any ship type we know of," the Captain said. "The beacon is damaged, but it could be a Terran ship, and by the treaty we are bound to assist Terran ships in distress."

P'Thok nodded. He remembered how pleased Matron Mi'Luki had been that the Terrans had also agreed to assist Treana'ad ships that were in distress.

"Is it answering hails?" P'Thok asked.

The Captain tapped his bladearms in negation. "No, Strike Leader. Which is why I summoned you."

P'Thok made a noise of agreement. "I shall get ready."

"Will you be taking the entire strike team?" the Captain asked.

P'Thok shook his head. "Only if needed. Have one of the engineers prepare, I may need his assistance should the engines prove damaged."

The Captain nodded, feeling better now that P'Thok was planning on handling it.

After all, hadn't P'Thok discovered the secrets that had allowed the Treana'ad people to flourish and overcome the deadly lemurs of Earth?

P'Thok adjusted the thrusters as he came in close to the strange ship. It looked mostly like a Terran ship, but the coloration was weird, the flashing lights were odd, and it was not responding to any hails. He could not see any damage, but P'Thok had been around enough to know that sometimes the most damaged ships looked perfectly intact from the outside.

He slowed down, hefting the magnetic grapple and firing it to help slow him even further. The monocable unspooled and the grapple hit, catching on a ferrous plate.

P'Thok held the handle of the pole, grabbing the handle of the crank, and rapidly turned the crank, pulling himself close to the ship. Once he reached it, he tapped the airlock control and waited. When nothing happened, he looked around and saw the plate covering the manual release.

Working quickly he opened the plate then braced himself, grabbing the handle on the wheel and slowly cranked the door open. He went inside the airlock and cranked it shut from inside.

The interior door opened smoothly and he found himself in a short hallway that looked like it met a central tube that obviously went from the airlock passage up to the nosecone. He could see the handles and foot steps so that he could move easily in the passage.

When he closed the airlock door and scuttled down to the middle tube.

P'Thok wasn't surprised when the gravity went to Zero-G as soon as he entered the tube.

He took a minute to orient himself. 'Below' him was another airlock, this one marked "Cargo Hold."

P'Thok nodded to himself. From where he had entered the ship, that meant that three quarters of its length was dedicated to cargo.

"P'Thok to *Glorious Trading Vessel*, P'Thok to *Glorious Trading Vessel*," P'Thok radioed.

He heard clicks and pops and realized they could not talk

RALTS BLOODTHORNE

back to him.

"I have boarded the Terran Republic Space Vessel *Rovaniemi* and am moving to investigate the bridge," P'Thok said. He looked around. The tube was covered with odd protrusions and was painted in a spiraling pattern of red and white. It wasn't that tall, maybe four times the height of a Treana'ad warrior.

P'Thok quickly climbed up and was almost halfway there when there was the clicking of relays and a rough voice, Terran but speaking perfect Treana'ad, echoed through the tube.

"It came without ribbons, it came without tags. It came without packages, boxes, or bags," the voice snarled. "Who attempts to stop me with malevolent glee?"

P'Thok looked at his suit. There were no ribbons on his suit. He had a nametag, but little else. He wasn't carrying anything.

"I am P'Thok, from the Treana'ad Space Faring Vessel *Glorious Trading Vessel*," the Treana'ad warrior answered. "I am here to provide assistance."

"Begone, you gigantic insectile pest," the unseen speaker said. "You can bring your vest, but you won't pass the test."

"Help me, mister P'Thok, for I am afraid!" P'Thok heard an immature voice cry out. "He's got a gun and a plan he has made!"

P'Thok had read the Republic codes and reviewed enough human media, as well as met enough humans, to know that what he was hearing was a little human girl, pre-pubescent, probably without all of her mastication dentition.

"Please, Mister P'Thok, help me, he kidnapped me from my bed after he gave me milk and cookies and patted my head!" the young human female's voice called out.

P'Thok pulled his plasma pistol free and hurried up the tube.

The lights at the sides of the tube began flashing and the walls of the tube began to rotate as tinkling music that was slightly upbeat began playing.

"My trap is clever and cruel," the male voice said. "Boarding my ship is something you'll rue!"

P'Thok adjusted his hat with one hand and pushed off of the

airlock door, floating upwards.

"You think you've beaten my swirly-hulry deadly murdly but our battle has yet to begin as we leave in a hurry!" the male voice said.

The ship began to vibrate and P'Thok found himself drifting back down as the ship began to move under its own power.

"Now you know not what to do as you discover the trap is for you!" the voice said.

"Oh, no, Mister P'Thok, because trouble I'm in," the little girl said. "How to help you, I don't know where to begin!"

P'Thok squinted, watching the way the steps and grips were moving. The swirl on the sides was interesting, but his compound eyes easily compensated for the movement. The footpads were steadily moving, the lights flashing, and the music was obviously supposed to be slightly disorienting.

But was he not P'Thok? Master of the agility tester and high scorer admired by warriors and ladies alike?

P'Thok adjusted his hat again, checked the charge on his pistol, and took the time to light a cigarette.

"Tobacco is bad for even bugs," the male voice said. "You'd be better off relying on hugs."

P'Thok swarmed up the tube, easily finding footing. It wasn't even as hard as the middle levels of the agility trainer machine, when you tested your footwork against a large green lemur with tusks.

"Your deceit and duplicity knows no bounds!" the voice said as P'Thok reached the airlock to the bridge. He slapped the open panel as the voice continued. "You cannot..."

P'Thok expected to see a human on the other side of the door.

The being on the other side of the door was tall, skinny, green furred, with burning yellow eyes, a tuft of mangy green hair on the top of the head, and long fingers. It looked weirdly greasy and abrasive at the same time and had a mouth full of yellow snaggly teeth that were somehow weirdly repellent to P'Thok. It had on a conical hat with a long tassel, made of red cloth, with

RALTS BLOODTHORNE

a white border on the creature's head and a white puffball at the end.

P'Thok had seen humans.

He knew it was no human.

He could see the immature female, wearing some kind of long clothing that was one piece, covered with a pattern of fruits and vegetables, her long yellow hair in curls and her blue eyes wide. She was tied to one of the chairs at the far left of the bridge.

"...save the girl or Christmas..." the creature said, the view-screen behind him showing the swirling colors of jumpspace.

P'Thok shot it through its open mouth and put two more shots into the creature's body.

It crashed to the ground, falling backwards into a box covered in bright and festive wrapping paper. The lid closed as P'Thok tossed an implosion grenade into the box.

The box vanished with a sucking sound, sparkles of proto-matter spinning and twirling in mid-air for a second before vanishing.

P'Thok turned to the little human female, spinning the plasma caster twice before holstering it.

"You all right, little lady?" He asked, using the Earthling drawl.

"Yes I am. Thank you, Mister P'Thok," the little girl said. When P'Thok cut her loose she jumped off the chair. She turned and looked at the screen. She pressed on a button that had a large visualization of a single flake of frozen water precipitation on it. "Hopefully we can go home where the ship can dock."

A large hologram appeared, distorted so it was too wide in the middle, only in red or white.

"Take the ship home, please, Babbo Natale?" the girl asked. "I really want to get home to my family."

"Ho... ho... ho..." the hologram said.

P'Thok nodded to himself. It was obviously trying to say the Terran word for home but was jammed up.

The little female child turned to P'Thok, facing the fearsome insectiod warrior. "The VI is broken and sad, we may be in trouble just a tad."

"Why did he tie you up?" P'Thok asked, moving up and looking at the controls. They looked fairly standard and he was trained in emergency piloting.

"My friends and I saved our local community center," the girl said. "He was going to build condos too expensive to be a renter."

"Oh," P'Thok said, not really understanding the child. "What's the cargo?"

"Presents and doodads and decorations galore," the girl said, hopping up and down. "Dollies and sleds and stockings and more!"

"Well, I'll see what I can do," P'Thok said. He stared at the controls. He was pretty sure what he needed to do.

He pressed the button and the ship dropped out of jump-space.

"Ho... ho... ho..." the VI said, obviously telling P'Thok it was trying to take them home.

The stars glimmered around them, a nearby nebula glowing softly.

BROUGHT TO YOU BY GURDY'S DUCK OIL AND DOCTOR GWARKARKAWT'S FOOT WEBBING CREAM! KEEP YOUR DUCK'S FEATHERS SOFT AND WATERPROOF WITH GURDY'S DUCK OIL AND THEM PADDLING HAPPILY WITH DOCTOR GWARKARKAWT'S PATENTED FOOT WEBBING CREAM!

Will P'Thok be able to pilot the ship? Will the girl get home in time to have roast beast? Who was that foul green creature?
For some of the answers and some other stuff, tune in next time!
Same P'Thok Time, Same P'Thok Channel!

MANTID FREE WORLDS

What are you showing the children?

---NOTHING FOLLOWS---

TREANA'AD HIVE WORLDS

How P'Thok Totally On Purpose and Not At All Accidentally Saved Christmas

---NOTHING FOLLOWS---

MANTID FREE WORLDS

Oh! I love this!

Move over, Cyb.

---NOTHING FOLLOWS---

comes with twelve genuine patented BobCo(TM) Just Add Water RealCows(TM), holographic Treana'ad moomoo carers with their own VI, and everything you see here! (batteries not included, please wait 4-12 hours for delivery)

Dee dee dah dee! It's BOOOOOOB-CO!

TELKAN FORGE WORLDS

Is it weird I want one?

---NOTHING FOLLOWS---

TREANA'AD HIVE WORLDS

Every time I see that had I have to remember they don't make those any more.

---NOTHING FOLLOWS---

CYBERNETIC ORGANISM CONSENSUS

Just fab one up. Templates are on SolNet.

---NOTHING FOLLOWS---

TREANA'AD HIVE WORLDS

It's just not the same. There's just something about BobCo stuff that templates don't replicate.

---NOTHING FOLLOWS---

PUBVIAN DOMINION

Cheapness?

TREANA'AD HIVE WORLDS

Don't be such a Grinch.

SIS! HURRY UP! IT'S ABOUT TO BE BACK ON!

There's just... you know... *something* about old BobCo stuff.

---NOTHING FOLLOWS---

MANTID FREE WORLDS

Don't start without me!

---NOTHING FOLLOWS---

We now return to the Sol System Broadcast Network Holiday Special, already in

PUBVIAN DOMINION

IT'S STARTING!

---NOTHING FOLLOWS---

MANTID FREE WORLDS

Whew. Made it.

Blow on it, it's hot.

---NOTHING FOLLOWS---

HAMAROOSA PINCHING TIME

What are the white things?

---NOTHING FOLLOWS---

BIOLOGICAL ARTIFICIAL SENTIENCE SYSTEMS

Marshmellows. Hush.

---NOTHING FOLLOWS---

in progress.

HOW P'THOK TOTALLY ON PURPOSE AND NOT AT ALL ACCIDENTALLY SAVED CHRISTMAS!

The spaceship was drifting as P'Thok looked at the unfamiliar controls. He'd only been on a few Terran ships, most of them captured military vessels, but he was pretty sure that none of them had control buttons and levers like this one.

Half of the buttons were different colored nubs with a clearish looking granular color. Most of the levers were colored with red and white spirals and either ended with a U or a wide multicolored disk. He wasn't precisely sure, but he was starting to think that there was something strange about the spaceship.

P'Thok adjusted his Moomoo tender hat and opened his faceplate, staring down at the controls.

His speed was five times a sparrow's flight but three seconds less than the day after tomorrow.

Chittering nervously he looked again. That made no sense, but he'd heard some Earthlings used bizarre measurements, but that was ridiculous.

"Mister P'Thok, I need to get back home and to my bed," the little Terran girl said. "After all, a Christmas story I've already been read."

"What was the cargo he was stealing so fast?" P'Thok asked. "I'm pretty sure the fuel in this ship isn't going to last?"

P'Thok frowned and tapped his translator. That last bit sounded weird.

"Presents and whizzbangs and tickle trikes for boys and girls galore," the girl said, kicking her feet where she was still in the chair. She was wearing a pink one piece suit with foot coverings that P'Thok had to admit looked pretty comfortable. Even the lace collar around her neck. "Fun stuff and neat stuff and some made with love not bought from a store."

"Umm, OK," P'Thok said. He looked at the navigation display. It had all of two markings on it. The ship, which was done in such a way that it looked like candy, and a star marked "Korvatunturi" underneath it.

P'Thok knew of most of the Terran settlements in the area. He'd just left New Terra with Moomoo's, ice cream, and tobacco, and there wasn't a Korvatunturi anywhere in the sector.

Maybe the ship had a new type of drive?

"I'm going to go check the drive. You stare here, little darling," P'Thok said, putting on his best Moomoo Carer Terran accent.

"I will Mister P'Thok. I'll watch the clock," she said, smiling.

P'Thok nodded and went back through the airlock. He hopped from outcropping to outcropping till he got to the bottom. He opened the next airlock and stared.

There were brightly colored packages, festooned with ribbons, everywhere he looked. They were piled haphazardly to the ceiling, in piles, and strewn about. There were large ornamented Terran foot coverings, laying on the floor, stuffed with toys and candy and fruit, some of them the contents spilling out onto the floor.

P'Thok held out his hand, catching a few flakes of frozen condensation on his palm.

The environmental system must be out, he thought to himself. He moved forward, skirting around the boxes and crates, the stockings and stuffings, even passed by a roast beast with all the trimmings that smelled delectable.

There were even evergreen trees festooned with decorations tossed here and there, complete with blinking lights and stars on top.

What primate madness have I found myself involved in? P'Thok wondered.

He passed several rows of compacted frozen precipitation that was fashioned into three spheres, each one smaller than the one beneath, stacked one on top of another. Each one had a black hat with a nifty brim that looked pretty spiffy to P'Thok, while others had small conical hats with a white puffball on the tip like the green thing had been wearing.

P'Thok grabbed one and shoved it in his pocket. Maybe the Matrons would like it.

At the back he opened the door to the engineering section, passing inside. He hit the lights and looked around.

There was fazoozals and caroozals, noomphy pumps and stungee dumps, marvelous condusers and fabulousa transoozters. There were wheedles wheedling and speedlings speeding. A whirling twirling jumping slumping spinning space of whirlamagig of contraptiopns and fantabulations.

P'Thok stared in shock.

Nothing he saw belonged in a spaceship engineering and drive room.

He wasn't even sure what any of it did, and he'd once stolen an armored ice cream transport.

He approached one of the many many many consoles, looking at the labels, which had such strange writing as "frosting thickening level thickener" and "creamy filling whipper stiller" and "choco-pecan-strawberry-injector".

The intercom clicked. "Is everything OK down there, Mr. P'Thok?" the little girl asked. "Of the equipment you should take stock."

"Um, everything's OK, small Terran female," he answered, looking around at everything.

He wasn't sure, but it looked like one of the wheels made of sugar and other ingredients had gotten slightly dislodged. He closed his eyes, took a deep breath, and pushed on it.

It clicked back in place and everything around him began moving. Some equipment whistled, others chimed a merry tune, and still more began turning or pumping or clacking or clanking.

P'Thok rushed out of the room and closed the door behind him, slumping against it and sighing. He brought out a cigarette and lit it, standing next to the stacked frozen water, and puffed at it.

"The tinsel drive is almost charged up," the little Earth girl said over the intercom. "I'm making cocoa would you like a cup?"

"Um, yes?" P'Thok said.

WE'LL BE RIGHT BACK AFTER THESE MESSAGES!

LEEBAW CONTEMPLATION POOL

Did this really happen?

---NOTHING FOLLOWS---

TREANA'AD HIVE WORLDS

Yes. And we'll fight anyone claims otherwise.

---NOTHING FOLLOWS---

LEEBAW CONTEMPLATION POOL

OK, OK, take it easy.

---NOTHING FOLLOWS---

TNVARU GRIPPING HANDS

I get it. This was made right after you guys encountered the Terrans, wasn't it?

---NOTHING FOLLOWS---

MANTID FREE WORLDS

Yes.

---NOTHING FOLLOWS---

TNVARU GRIPPING HANDS

And you guys didn't really have any culture beyond "Must Lay Eggs!" and "Please don't eat my head!"

---NOTHING FOLLOWS---

PUBVIAN DOMINION

>Laughs

Yeah, that was pretty much them.

---NOTHING FOLLOWS---

TNVARU GRIPPING HANDS

I totally get it. Matron Sangbre and Matron Nakteti are making a movie based on when they met Daxin and how they got to Earth. This is kind of like that.

---NOTHING FOLLOWS---

HAKANIAN FLOOF ZONE

Woah, check it out! A hoverbike with a radio, jet boosters, max ceiling of three hundred meters and autopilot!
I totally want one!

---NOTHING FOLLOWS---

MANTID FREE WORLDS

They don't make them any more. Too many kids slammed into each other or sucked birds into the intakes and crashed or flew into orbit somehow.

---NOTHING FOLLOWS---

HAKANIAN FLOOF ZONE

Wait, those are for kids?
Who the hell gives kids something like that.
ALL>TERRANS!
ALL>laughs

MANTID FREE WORLDS

Hush, it's back on.

---NOTHING FOLLOWS---

WE NOW RETURN TO THE HOLIDAY SPECIAL, ALREADY IN PROGRESS

P'Thok exhaled the last of the smoke out of feet, ignoring that it made perfect smoke rings, and moved back through the cargo area. In several places large dolls of small Terrans with pointed ears watched him, their outfits brightly colored and festive looking.

When he got to the bridge he looked around. The tiny human female gave him a large mug, hot to the touch, with whipped cream on top.

"Mister P'Thok, I made you a drink, you will like it I think," the human child said.

"Thank you, tiny human," P'Thok said.

The controls were all lit up and one big button was flashing.

P'Thok moved up and stared at it, watching it flash. Idly he took a sip of the hot drink.

It was pleasant to the taste, reminding him of a heated bowl of Choco-Marshmallow Flavor Bomb Ice Cream. He took another drink, gave the equivelant of a shrug, and pressed the big red button.

The ship flew into motion. P'Thok shot backward, the mug in his hand leaving behind a long trail of whipped cream and hot chocolate, until he hit the back wall with an "OOF!" noise. Sparkles and small birds appeared around his head for a moment until he shook his head.

The ship picked up speed and P'Thok felt the chitin on his face began to ripple and pull backwards, deforming his head. It wasn't painful, but he could see his reflection and it looked like his mandibles were flapping.

The ship suddenly came to a stop and P'Thok flew through the bridge to slam against the viewsceen, all sprawled out, a leg or arm in every direction, still holding onto his mug of liquid choco-bomb.

He slowly slid down with a squeaking noise and landed on the floor.

The ship was making a beeping sound and P'Thok got to his feet, took another drink to calm his nerves, and looked at the panel and the viewscreen.

A large planet, all white and blue, with clouds swirling around, was getting closer.

"Oh no, Mister P'Thok, the controls have gone out," the tiny Terran girl said. "If I can't get home my parents will shout."

P'Thok stared at the instruments. "I'm not sure what to do."

The little girl pointed a long braid of multicolored ribbon twined with shiny metallic silver threads. "You'll have to take that, go out on the hull, lasso the cosecone, then give it a pull."

"I'll burn up on reentry," P'Thok said.

The little girl picked up the vanished green creature's red hat with the white fluffy border and white puffball on the tip. "Wear the Gurnch's magical hat, it will protect you from heat and things like that!"

P'Thok sighed, moved over and picked up the hat, and swapped it out for his moomoo tender hat. It fit comfortably between his antenna sheathes on his spacesuit helmet.

"All right. We're falling fast," P'Thok said. "I'll go out and pull the nose up on the ship."

"And then we'll land and be done with part of the trip," the little human female said.

P'Thok moved back into the central traverse tube, checking the long strand of ribbon and silver metal.

He'd practiced the art of lassoing moomoos on his own world, so he let the large loop fall out of the coil of rope, moving to the airlock.

It had power, allowing him to cycle it and go outside.

The ship was heading toward the planet, falling nose first.

P'Thok clumped outside the ship, his magnetic boots making it so he had to walk slow, stiltingly. He got halfway forward and let the lasso fall.

The ship was starting to enter atmosphere, heat from reentry making the round ball at the end of the nosecone glow a bright red.

P'Thok twirled the lasso over his head and let it fly, compensating for the pull of the planet and the thin atmospheric drag. The end of the lasso widened out and dropped over the nosecone, and P'Thok pulled back, expecting nothing.

The nose slowly began to rise as the ship dropped into atmosphere, rapidly dropping. P'Thok held onto the rope, pulling tight, like he was trying to get a meanmoomoo to stop.

Fire roared around the strangely shaped ship as it dropped into atmosphere, heading for the snowy expanse of trees on the surface. The ship left behind tree shaped puffs of white smoke as it fell to the ground, surrounded by fire.

Finally the ship slammed into the snow and P'Thok was thrown from the ship, flailing through the air, giving out a strange cry of "YA-HOO-HOO-HOOEY!" before landing in the snow and making a perfect Treana'ad shaped hole.

WILL P'THOK SURVIVE? WHAT SECRETS ARE IN THE BOXES? WILL THE TERRAN GRUB GET HOME?
YOU'LL FIND OUT, RIGHT AFTER THESE COMMERCIALS!

AKLTAK SOARING WORLDS

This is so exciting, I don't even care that there's no way a 'magic hat' would keep him from burning up on reentry.

---NOTHING FOLLOWS---

TREANA'AD HIVE WORLDS

I know, isn't it great?

---NOTHING FOLLOWS---

HAKANIAN GESTALT THINGY

So what's on after this?

---NOTHING FOLLOWS---

MANTID FREE WORLDS

Um...

Puffies in Winter Wonderland.

Aw. I always cry during that. I'll be bawling again, only for a different reason.

---NOTHING FOLLOWS---

PUBVIAN DOMINION

You guys still watch that?

Wow.

---NOTHING FOLLOWS---

TREANA'AD HIVE WORLDS

Sis loves it.

---NOTHING FOLLOWS---

MANTID FREE WORLDS

After that is...

Oh, wow, they're really pulling out the old ones.

AKLTAK SOARING WORLDS

What?

---NOTHING FOLLOWS---

They're pulling out "Daxin & KISS Save Santa."

---NOTHING FOLLOWS---

TNVARU GRIPPING HANDS

THAT SOUNDS AMAZING!

Wait, what's KISS?

---NOTHING FOLLOWS---

TREANA'AD HIVE WORLDS

A heavy metal band that's been going for like 9,000 years. They've had like 500 band members over the centuries.

Check out this picture.

---NOTHING FOLLOWS---

TNVARU GRIPPING HANDS

They look scary. Is that guy breathing fire? And what's wrong with his tongue?

---NOTHING FOLLOWS---

PUBVIAN DOMINION

Don't ask.

They're STILL around?

---NOTHING FOLLOWS---

MANTID FREE WORLDS

Yeah. They released an album like last year.

---NOTHING FOLLOWS---

HAKANIAN FUZZY TOWN

OK, tell me that they didn't really give kids what's in this commercial.

A BobCo Anti-Grav belt? Really?

---NOTHING FOLLOWS---

DIGITAL ARTIFICIAL SENTIENCE SYSTEMS

Oh yes, yes they did.

---NOTHING FOLLOWS---

HAKANIAN FUZZY TOWN

That just seems so dangerous.

---NOTHING FOLLOWS---

BIOLOGICAL ARTIFICIAL SENTIENCE SYSTEMS

You've MET humans, right?

Someday allow me to explain the concept of "Lawn Dart" to you.

---NOTHING FOLLOWS---

TELKAN FORGE WORLDS

Oh, I so want one of those.

Ten Thousand and One Science Experiments! Now with Uranium-238!

That'll help our scientists!

---NOTHING FOLLOWS---

PUBVIAN DOMINION

You realize that's for kids, right?

And made by BobCo.

---NOTHING FOLLOWS---

TELKAN FORGE WORLDS

Wait, they're giving kids radioactive material to do experiments with?

What kind of psycho does that?

---NOTHING FOLLOWS---

ALL> BOOOOOOOB-CO!

ALL>LAUGH

MANTID FREE WORLDS

Hush, it's back on.

---NOTHING FOLLOWS---

We now return you to the SolNet Holiday Special, already in progress!

P'Thok stuck his head out of the hole he'd left, shaking his head to clear the snow from over his eyes and hanging off his chin. It took two tries, but he managed to do it. He reached up and touched his face, realizing that somehow he'd lost his helmet.

Well, at least he still had the 'magic' red hat.

He climbed out of the snow, taking time to shake off.

He blinked at the ship, where it was just laying in the snow, like nothing had happened. The little human girl was standing outside the ship, hugging herself tightly.

"Mister P'Thok, I fear it's a bit chilly," the immature human female said. "We don't have time to be a little silly."

"Right. I'll try to figure out..." P'Thok started to say.

A large animal, with huge horns and thick brown fur and four legs rather than the proper six, burst from the snow covered shrubs, followed by nearly a dozen more, all pulling an ornate red and white conveyance decorated with brass, shining silver, and more of the white and red striped bars.

Driving it was a Rigellian female, wearing fluffy red pants

with white fur at the waist and the ankles, a set of cross chest leather straps dyed in white and red stripes, large black boots, and a hat like P'Thok had on his head on her head.

"I saw your ship and came as fast I could," the Rigellian called out, standing up and snapping a whip covered with bells that made a tinkling sound as she cracked it over the animal's horns. "I brought the sleigh like I promised I would."

P'Thok noticed her features were strange. She had a cleft chin, heavy brow, patrician nose, and her coloring was slightly off, looking more greenish gray than greyish green.

"Hanna Somme!" the Terran girl squealed, clapping her hands. P'Thok noticed she had pulled on mittens when he wasn't looking. "but we should call you SqueeWark."

The Rigellian female reigned in the prancing quadruped beasts, the leather straps attaching them all tinkling and winking as bells and lights danced.

"I have come to help the two of you with the work," Hanna Somme said.

P'Thok tapped his translator. That one sounded weird.

"Let us unpack the ship of presents and gifts," Hanna Somme SqueeWark said, adjusting her hat. "Luckily great weight I can lift."

P'Thok waded through the snow as the side of the ship lowered to reveal all of the brightly colored packages. Hanna got out, adjusting her thick shiny black belt, moving next to the spaceship. P'Thok moved up next to the Rigellian female as the little Terran female handed Hanna a package, who handed it to P'Thok, who stacked it in the back of the animal pulled sleigh.

WE WILL BE RIGHT BACK AFTER THESE MESSAGES!

PUBVIAN DOMINION

You know it only went to commercial so we don't have to watch them work.

---NOTHING FOLLOWS---

MANTID FREE WORLDS

Shush, don't spoil it for the children.

---NOTHING FOLLOWS---

TNVARU GRIPPING HANDS

Why is this Terran woman describing loneliness?

Oh. If I feel that way, I should call others or visit them?

What if I don't have family?

---NOTHING FOLLOWS---

LEEBAW CONTEMPLATION POOL

Oh, we can call her or another Terran via SolNet, free, and talk to them.

I think I'd like that. It's been kind of scary lately.

---NOTHING FOLLOWS---

MANTID FREE WORLDS

You aren't alone any more, dears.

---NOTHING FOLLOWS---

HAKANIAN FUZZY GESTALT THINGAMABOB

Oh, more toys.

What happened to BobCo?

---NOTHING FOLLOWS---

TREANA'AD HIVE WORLDS

They were based on Pubvia. They moved there only a few decades before the war. They got glassed like Pubvia did and...

wait...

---NOTHING FOLLOWS---

PUBVIAN DOMINION

Wait? What?

BobCo is here?

---NOTHING FOLLOWS---

TELKAN FORGE WORLDS

HE'S GOT BOBCO MERCH! GET HIM!

---NOTHING FOLLOWS---

TREANA'AD HIVE WORLDS

TURN HIM UPSIDE DOWN AND SHAKE HIM!

---NOTHING FOLLOWS---

MANTID FREE WORLDS

Will you two stop that?

Presents aren't going to fall out of his pockets.

Wait, is that a RealDog Robofriend(TM)?

SHAKE HIM HARDER!

---NOTHING FOLLOWS---

We now return to your holiday special, already in

RIGELLIAN SAURIAN COMPACT

Settle down, it's starting again.

---NOTHING FOLLOWS---

progress.

Holding on his hat with one hand, P'Thok looked behind him at the back of the sled and shook his head. The brightly wrapped boxes were piled into a huge stack that gravity and physics said must fall over at any second, but there it was, wobbling back and forth, once in a while decorative glass balls or large snowflakes flying off it.

Hanna Somme cracked her whip over the draft beasts as they charged through the snow, toward a large structure.

"If we can get safely to the top, we can make sure the presents are delivered to all the good girls and boys," the little Terran female said. "We'll deliver the stockings, cookies, treats, surprises, and toys."

P'Thok nodded, staring at the large building. It was round, with a crenelated top. It looked fairly ominous and P'Thok was more than a little worried about it.

Still, the Rigellian female was an expert at driving the conveyance, he had to admit. She deftly weaved between the trees, large snowdrifts, and stacked up balls of snow with crude faces made with black rock smiles and eyes and some kind of long thin orange tuber for a nose.

"There's a light on..." the little Terran female grub began to sing.

"Over at the Nahktomee Place," the Rigellian sang.

"There's a light on," P'Thok pointed out as a single window lit up with orange flickering light.

"Burning in the fireplace," the Rigellian female sang/answered.

"There's a light, light in the darkness of everybody's life," the Terran grub sang.

P'Thok shook his head as the other two kept singing as they drove through the snow filled night. He had heard Rigellians were a musical people and he had to admit, she had a nice voice.

The song went on and on as they headed toward the tall round building.

The red and white sleigh slowed down in front of the tower, coming to stop at the loading dock.

"Here we have arrived after a brisk sleigh ride," the Rigellian said.

"I'm almost home to my bed," the Terran grub said, "I'm all warm and toasty and fed."

P'Thok looked up at the building. It was made of slightly reflective clear crysteel and endosteel. A modern building with all the trimmings, complete with blinking lights at the top.

The Rigellian beeped a horn that sounded musical and cheery.

After a few moments the door slid open and the Rigellian cracked her whip, driving the twelve plus one beasts into the large garage. There were miniature Terrans inside, with wide eyes, pointed ears, sharp chins, and festive looking clothing. They quickly began to unload the packages, throwing them into tubes that pulled the cargo packages up into the tube with the characteristic "whoosh" of grav-lift.

They were almost done, in the time it took P'Thok to blink twice, when the lid of a box popped off. The furry green creature lunged up out of the box, grabbed the Terran grub with two long arms.

"You thought you were all free," the green thing said. "But you have no killed me!"

"Oh, no, it's the Grunch!" the Rigellian exclaimed, putting one forearm against her forehead and collapsing back slightly. "He'll eat Windy-Wu for lunch!"

"At the top of the tower I'll be," the green furry thing said as it did a somersault in place and dropped inside the box. "You must duel to set Windy-Wu free!"

P'Thok ran up and looked into the box, seeing nothing but a

plas bottom.

"How many times do I have to kill that thing?" he asked, straightening up.

"It serves the Goobers, who everyone does fear," Hanna said. "I'll wait with the sleigh and stay right here."

P'Thok sighed, walking toward the elevator.

When he got inside he looked at the buttons for a moment. There were tons of them, all looking like white disks with red spiral lines. Looking at it, he decided to press the only one that had green swirls instead of red.

Sighing again, P'Thok leaned against the elevator wall, pulling out his two plasma caster pistols and checking them over. One was damaged, the barrel spitting sparks. The other was almost depleted. Only a few rounds left.

He checked his hold-out, a nifty Terran slug caster, made of shiny endosteel and embellished with bronze, he'd picked up, where he'd hidden it in his right foreboot.

For a second he wondered when he'd taken off his spacesuit, then shrugged. It didn't matter. He took the slug caster and tucked it behind his back where it wasn't immediately obvious.

Finally the elevator dinged and the door slid open slowly.

The room was lit by a cozy fire in a fireplace, with pillars holding up the ceiling and festive decorations scattered about, including a tree that had been hauled in doors and decorated.

Ahead of him, by the window that had the storm shutter rolled up, was the furry green thing and a tall Terran male all dressed in black.

"So you're the one out to stop me from stealing Christmas from all," the Terran said.

"I told you when I came back that he answered the girl's call," the green thing said, pointing at the Terran grub being held tightly by the tall Terran.

"Mister P'Thok help me please," the grub said. "Without presents happiness will cease."

"Let the girl go," P'Thok said, slowly moving forward and gauging the distance.

"Our answer is no," the green thing said.

"Don't say I didn't give you warning most true," P'Thok said. He looked down and tapped his translator.

"Say what you want there's nothing you can do," the green thing said, chuckling.

"Your plasma pistol throw it here," the male said. He shook the little Terran grub, who cried out. "Or I'll harm what you hold dear."

"Don't trust Hansel's words, Mister P'Thok," the grub said. "The Goober boys lie when they talk."

P'Thok drew his plasma pistol with two fingers before tossing it to the green thing.

He saw that both the Terran and the green thing were watching the plasma pistol fly through the air.

He had practiced the maneuver repeatedly after seeing a Terran bodyguard perform it.

P'Thok pulled the slug thrower from behind his back, firing rapidly. Four shots to the green thing, since three didn't do it last time, two shots into the tall human, center of the upper chest, above Windy-Wu's head.

The bullets went through the green thing, which slowly collapsed like a pricked balloon, shattering the window behind them.

The tall Terran male staggered backwards, still holding onto the little Terran grub. P'Thok rushed forward, grabbing the Terran grub with his gripping hands and pushing the Terran's arms away with this bladearms.

His instinct was to stab the Terran male, but he didn't have a good angle as the Terran male staggered back, still holding onto Windy-Wu. P'Thok pulled backwards, making the little Terran grub cry out in pain.

The Terran male stepped too far backwards, overbalancing, falling out of the window. He grabbed little Windy-Wu's hat, holding tight, even as he dropped. The grub gagged and choked, the string at the bottom cutting into her neck.

P'Thok pulled on the little girl, lifting her up, one bladearm moving to slice through the string.

The Terran male fell, waving his arms, vanishing into the snow for a moment before there was a sudden explosion that showered up sparkles and spinning lights.

"Thank You Mister P'Thok, for all you have did," the grub said. "You saved me, a cute little kid."

"Yeah, yeah, kid," P'Thok said. He turned and picked up his plasma pistol before carrying the grub to the elevator. "Let's find out what else needs did."

P'Thok looked down at his translator and shook his head.

The elevator door closed with a ping.

WE'LL BE RIGHT BACK AFTER THESE MESSAGES!

MANTID FREE WORLDS

It's just not Christmas without Hansel Goober falling from the Tower of Nahktomee.

---NOTHING FOLLOWS---

...gen-you-wine BobCo Dehydrated Moomoo farm! Use only with parental permission. Allow 4-12 hours for delivery! Trained praying mantis moomoo tenders included! Buy in the next 15 minutes and get a genuine P'Thok Chee-chee-chee-chia Pet! Operators are standing by!

Only from... BOOOOooooB-CO!

TREANA'AD HIVE WORLDS

Oh God, I want one so bad. All of me wants one! IT'S SO AMAZING!

---NOTHING FOLLOWS---

TELKAN FORGE WORLDS

So, a Chia-Pet is just a clay bust of P'Thok that you smear gel containing grass seeds on and it grows green grass like hair?

But that's stupid, P'Thok didn't have hair...

---NOTHING FOLLOWS---

TREANA'AD HIVE WORLDS

YOU SHUT UP!

DAMMIT! WE'RE RUBBING OUR CREDIT CARDS ON THE SCREEN AND NOTHING IS HAPPENING!

---NOTHING FOLLOWS---

AKLTAK SOARING WORLDS

Does he get like this every time he sees these commercials?

---NOTHING FOLLOWS---

ALL> YES!

ALL> Laughs

PUBVIAN DOMINION

Wow.

---NOTHING FOLLOWS---

MANTID FREE WORLDS

What?

---NOTHING FOLLOWS---

PUBVIAN DOMINION

So, like a half hour ago I sent people to check out the BobCo facility.

Apparently it's operational.

---NOTHING FOLLOWS---

BIOLOGICAL ARTIFICIAL SENTIENCE SYSTEMS

What?

It's what?

---NOTHING FOLLOWS---

PUBVIAN DOMINION

Apparently it's up and running, producing toys right now.

The four LawSec and two government officials received gifts that they're blasting all over social media right now.

The Treana'ad ambassador who arrived last week was just gifted a "Genuine BobCo Autonomous Animatronic Moomoo" by the BobCo AI. Not a digital sentience, an actual AI. The Ambassador is taking vids of him petting his Moomoo and having it do tricks. He's lording it over every other Treana'ad in existence by posting it to the Smokey Cone diplomatic site.

The Treana'ad Matron in charge of the diplomatic team received a P'Thok ChiaPet, a fishtank full of Genuine Sea Monkeys, a Robotic Nanite Circus of Wonders, two minature RealMoomoos(TM), and a Genuine BobCo HoloHat.

She's currently talking to the hive matrons on Smokey Cone wearing the Holohat and petting her minature moomoos on the video conference to the other matrons.

I think one is frothing at the mouth in envy.
I better get a hand on this before there's a riot.
---NOTHING FOLLOWS---
TREANA'AD> SCREAMS IN FRUSTRATION

HAMAROOSA PINCHING CHAIN LETTER
Is he going to be like this every commercial?
He's not going to have a stroke, is he?
---NOTHING FOLLOWS---

DIGITAL ARTIFICIAL SENTIENCE SYSTEMS
Wait, the BobCo AI is online?
---NOTHING FOLLOWS---

TNVARU GRIPPING HANDS
I thought AI was a racial slur?
---NOTHING FOLLOWS---

DIGITAL ARTIFICIAL SENTIENCE SYSTEMS
It is. But the BobCo AI is... well... let's just say it's unique.
---NOTHING FOLLOWS---

MANTID FREE WORLDS
And homicidal.
---NOTHING FOLLOWS---

DIGITAL ARTIFICIAL SENTIENCE SYSTEMS
Oh yes. Definitely homicidal.
---NOTHING FOLLOWS---

TREANA'AD HIVE WORLDS
OH MY GOD THE BOBCO SOLNET STOREFRONT WORKS!
SQUEEEEEEEEEEEEE
asdfasdfasdf7as9df79aspdufhasdkjfn   nkjq234q8fa9sd-
fYAU(*&*&S^D*D&FYkaujshdjfahas
>USER TREANA'AD HIVE WORLDS HAS LEFT THE CHAT (SQUEE
OUT OF RANGE)

CYBERNETIC ORGANISM COOPERATIVE
AHAHAHAHAHHA!
He crashed his interface.
---NOTHING FOLLOWS---

LEEBAW CONTEMPLATION POOL
Wait, if it's homicidal, why isn't anyone worried?

---NOTHING FOLLOWS---

MANTID FREE WORLDS

Because technically it isn't an AI or a Digital Sentience or even a digitized Terran.

It's this weird blending of the two.

---NOTHING FOLLOWS---

CLONE WORLDS CONSORTIUM

Because Bob "Caveman" Johnson was a complete psycho.

---NOTHING FOLLOWS---

MANTID FREE WORLDS

Technically, he wasn't a psychopath. He was just... over-imaginative with a lack of ethics and morals in some specific areas.

---NOTHING FOLLOWS---

CLONE WORLDS CONSORTIUM

Like combining Mantid and Terran DNA to create mantis-men supersoldiers to guard his toy shipments?

---NOTHING FOLLOWS---

MANTID FREE WORLDS

Yeah, like that.

---NOTHING FOLLOWS---

TNVARU GRIPPING HANDS

That seems... psychotic.

---NOTHING FOLLOWS---

LEEBAW CONTEMPLATION POOL

He's been gone for a while. Is he going to be OK?

---NOTHING FOLLOWS---

RIGELLIAN SAURIAN COMPACT

He's a little busy. The BobCo SolNet "Always Online(TM)" store is so overloaded it's actually reverted to a 2.5D storefront with limited interaction.

AHA!

They DO still sell Fantabulosa Pond Paddling No-Windup(TM) Squeaky Ducklings that sing over 100 duckling songs.

OUT OF STOCK!

Dammit, there was 1.2 million left when I read that out loud, now it's "Temporarily Out of Stock".

Oh, hey, I get a free sixty four ounce container of BobCo Muscle-Max Ultra Sick Gains Powder for my trouble.
Score!

---NOTHING FOLLOWS---

TELKAN FORGE WORLDS

About that AI...

---NOTHING FOLLOWS---

MANTID FREE WORLDS

It's complicated. It's a cross between programmed AI, one of the first baked hash shredded rainbow salted table genesis systems, and a neural recording of Bob Johnson himself all mushed together.

---NOTHING FOLLOWS---

PUBVIAN DOMINION

And just as crazy as the original Bob Johnson.

---NOTHING FOLLOWS---

MANTID FREE WORLDS

How can you tell? He's a human. They're all crazy.

---NOTHING FOLLOWS---

RRA S

an hear you out th

////

ROONALT N'KGEST

0773H??

-WOL-S-NOFOL-GNIT----

MANTID FREE WORLDS

Everyone settle down! We've got a new one.

---NOTHING FOLLOWS---

>TREANA'AD HIVE WORLDS (IT'S A BOBCO CHRISTMAS!) has logged on

MANTID FREE WORLDS

Come over here, sweety. Let big sister help you sort it out.
You can watch Tri-Vid with the rest of us.

N'KAROO MIND DATALINK GESTALT I/O SYSTEM BOOTSTRAP
um ok

///END OUTPUT AWAITING INPUT

We now return to: How P'Thok Totally On Purpose and Not At All Accidentally Saved Christmas.

The little Terran immature female held tightly to P'Thok's right foreleg, looking up with wide frightened eyes.

"Mister P'Thok, there were plans I fear," she said. P'Thok tapped his translator. "The Goober Boys kidnapped Baby New Year!"

"The who did what now?" P'Thok asked.

A bright colored paper wrapped package quivered, the lid shot off, sparkles and confetti shot out, and the sides fell down to reveal an infant Terran male wearing a tall cylinderical black hat with a wide brim, a diaper, and a sash that said "HAPPY NEW YEAR" in holographic letters that scrolled around the sash.

"He's the one who rings in the New Year with a bow!" Little Windy-Wu said.

"HAPPY NEW YEAR!" the baby crowed out in a high pitched voice.

P'Thok just shrugged, figuring his translator had given it up, then moved over and picked up the human infant, who held his arms up in eagerness to be picked up.

"Let's get the two of you back to the sled so we can get you both home and to bed," P'Thok said, maneuvering around the flickering fires and the puddles of water.

The elevator gave a cheery ding and P'Thok got into it, surprised when less than a second later the door opened and he found himself on the ground floor again. The Rigellian female was sitting in the red sleigh, waving him over. P'Thok ran through the snow, spraying up a wave on either side of him as he hurried over, and stopped next to the sleigh.

"HAPPY NEW YEAR!" the infant crowed out.

"The children should be home all snug in their beds," he said. "With visions of sugar-plums and ice cream dancing in their heads."

P'Thok tapped his translator again.

"Climb aboard and let us be off," the Rigellian sang/spoke. "We'll get there with nary a sneeze or a cough!"

P'Thok climbed on board, holding tight to the two Terran children.

Windy-Wu gave a large yawn and rubbed her equally large eyes. The infant laughed and clapped his hands with glee as the Rigellian shook the reins and the sleigh suddenly flew over the trees. P'Thok held on as tight as can be, looking around to see what he could see. Through the air they flew as fast as a sparrow, the Hannah Somme SqueeWark keeping the path straight as an arrow.

"Oh Dasher, Oh Dancer, Oh Smasher and Fixins! On Comment, on Stupid, on Ronald and Fitzen! Dash away dash away dash away all!" the Rigellian sang out as P'Thok reached up and held tight to his moomoo carer hat with one bladearm, holding the children close with his hands so they could stay warm.

"HAPPY NEW YEAR!" the baby yelled out.

"To the top of the roof, to the top of the mall, crash away smash away bash away all!" the Rigellian sang. She turned to P'Thok. "Start throwing out the presents for good little girls and boys, we have much to deliver, all presents and toys."

"Um, OK," P'Thok turned and looked at the back of the sleigh. He chittered in anxious shock when he saw there were miniature humans with huge eyes and pointed ears and beards all attaching balloons to the brightly wrapped gifts. He was handed one and curious, he tossed it up. The balloon caught the wind and flew away, dancing on the winter wind, beeping a tune as it made it way.

P'Thok kept tossing balloon lifted presents out the back, even as Windy-Wu covered herself and the wide-eyed infant with a red blanket with white fuzzy trim. They flew into the night, setting presents aloft to go where they may, the Rigellian, the Treana'ad, the immature human and the tiny baby.

We Will Return Right After These Messages!

CYBERNETIC ORGANISM CONSENSUS

You aren't going to have a stroke, are you?

---NOTHING FOLLOWS---

TREANA'AD HIVE WORLDS

I don't think so.

Wow. When I realized I could order a dehydrated moomoo farm everything kind of gets hazy.

---NOTHING FOLLOWS---

DIGITAL ARTIFICIAL SENTIENCE SYSTEMS

Man, BobCo had you guys hooked, didn't they?

---NOTHING FOLLOWS---

BIOLOGICAL ARTIFICIAL SENTIENCE SYSTEMS

Like you have any room to talk.

---NOTHING FOLLOWS---

DIGITAL ARTIFICIAL SENTIENCE SYSTEMS

I was never that bad.

---NOTHING FOLLOWS---

MANTID FREE WORLDS

Less than a dozen words.

"BobCo Full eVR Twenty Flags Self-Learning Procedurally Generated Amusement Park"

---NOTHING FOLLOWS---

DIGITAL ARTIFICIAL SENTIENCE SYSTEMS

WHERE?

IT'S MINE!

I SAW IT FIRST!

---NOTHING FOLLOWS---

ALL> LAUGH

DIGITAL ARTIFICIAL SENTIENCE SYSTEMS

OK, fair point.

---NOTHING FOLLOWS---

LEEBAW CONTEMPLATION POOL

Wait, they have an entire section of their merchandise store entirely devoted to amphibians and amphibious reptiles?

---NOTHING FOLLOWS---

PUBVIAN DOMINION

Yup.

---NOTHING FOLLOWS---

LEEBAW CONTEMPLATION POOL

Well, since they never met us I doubt they'll have anything we'd be interested in. These are probably tailored specifically to you... Is that a self-installing seasonally adaptive micro-ecology relaxation pool with a water fall and real plants? Wow! Bio-luminescent fish! Hypo-allergenic pollywogs and musical singing frogs! Glittersand? Wow! That looks amazing? Holy crap, only three easy payments?

OH MY GOD THEY'RE STILL IN STOCK!

MY ORDER WENT THROUGH FOR WORMHOLE DELIVERY! IT'LL BE HERE IN ONLY A FEW HOURS!

---NOTHING FOLLOWS---

TREANA'AD HIVE WORLDS

LOL Owned

---NOTHING FOLLOWS---

We now return you to our scheduled program, brought to you by Dolly Parton-Madison Cupcakes and Children's Books in partnership with Mi'Luki Genuine Moo-Moo Milk Ice Cream!

P'Thok tossed the last present out and leaned back. His arms and shoulders, even his bladearm shoulders, were aching with the effort, but at last the back of the sleight was empty, only a sleeping miniature human curled up under and empty bag made of red cloth with white fuzz.

"It's almost midnight, Mister P'Thok," Windy-Wu yawned. "We have to get Baby New Year home and beat the clock."

The Rigellian female nodded, snapping the reins, and P'Thok felt himself pushed back by the sudden accelleration. His chitin began to ripple and flap like rubber as the wind whipped by and the stars blurred, undergoing color-shift due to the speed.

"HAPPY NEW YEAR!" the baby yelled out again. P'Thok looked at it, shaking his head and wondering if all Terran infants were so loud.

The sleigh slowed down, descending rapidly, to splash into the snow, coming to a stop, the reindeer standing relaxed and placidly.

"We're here," Windy-Wu said, pointing at a brightly lit shack. "They're there."

The snow exploded next to P'Thok and a furry green creature, lean and evil, with glowing yellow eyes, popped out of the snow.

"I'M EVERYWHERE!" it roared.

"IT'S THE GRUNCH!" cried out SqeeWark, putting her forearm to her forehead and collapsing back in a near faint, her oiled muscles rippling in the light from the cabin as her eyelashes fluttered in a near faint.

"You can run near and far," the Grunch said, capering about in the snow, "I'll stick with you like shoes and tar."

"How many times do I have to kill this thing?" P'Thok asked, pulling out his pistol and firing five times, since four didn't seem to work.

"It can only be defeated if we sing!" Windy-Wu warned.

"HAPPY NEW YEAR!" the infant repeated, hitting P'Thok on the side of the head with a rattle.

P'Thok jumped out, chasing after the green thing as it capered through the snow, diving into large drifts only to peek around a tree meters and make faces at P'Thok. The plasma pistols fired sparkles and sparklers, quarkers and barklers, spinners and grinners, and whirring plasmaglobers.

Windy-Wu and Hannah Somme began to sing as P'Thok chased it. Once the Grunch threw down a dark circle at its feet, jumping in and vanishing, only to reappear on the other side of the clearing, leering at P'Thok from behind a tree. P'Thok followed and dropped into a snowbank, managing to pop off a shot at the Grunch that hit it in the buttocks, making it screech and run around in circles, trying to put out the fur that had caught on fire.

As P'Thok struggled out of the snowdrift the Grunch put its buttocks in the snow, a cloud of garlic smelling steam billowing up. By the time P'Thok got over to the cloud, the Grunch was gone. P'Thok came around the corner and the Grunch was holding up a picture frame.

"Wait, P'Thok, you should see how you look," the Grunch said, holding up the picture frame in front of his own face. "You should see yourself like the children I took!"

P'Thok frowned, moving closer, wondering why the Grunch was holding up an empty picture frame in front of his own face.

Before P'Thok could ask a question the Grunch punched him in the face, making stars and tweeting birds appear over P'Thok's head. The Grunch gave a laugh and dove into the snow, reappearing on the roof where he capered and danced doncha know?

"Mister Grunch, there's a gift left!" Windy-Wu called, holding up the almost empty bag.

The Grunch stopped dancing and moved slowly up to the sleigh. P'Thok leaned against the tree gasping and wishing he hadn't skipped leg day.

Windy-Wu pulled out a gift, giving it to the Grunch, who was only used to other people's half eaten thrown away lunch. He unwrapped it, his face all sour, he expected nothing, his Christmas was dour.

A sparkling orange did appear, held aloft by the Grinch, who'd been naughty all year. A small gift it was, but chosen with care, by Windy-Wu, and Baby New Year.

The Grunch felt his heart swell three times right there, he grabbed Windy-Wu while P'Thok stood and stared.

"I no longer feel bad, I feel only good," the Grunch exclaimed, as P'Thok aimed his pistol at the back of his head.

P'Thok pulled the trigger, expecting a plasma shot, but got only a jaunty tune instead.

'And you, P'Thok, who discovered ice cream so yummy," the Grunch said, cartwheeling and somersaulting to where the Treana'ad stood. "I have for you something for your tummy."

It was a mug of hot chocolate, a warm drink for the cold. The Grunch gave it to P'Thok for the warrior to hold.

The door of the cabin opened wide and a woman waved them inside. P'Thok followed them all, wondering what was next with a sigh.

The cabin was cheery, decorated and warm, with cookies and moomoo milk and ice cream galore. The Grunch cut the roast beast, Windy-Wu yawned and began to snore.

At the stroke of midnight baby New Year laughed and sparkles filled the air.

"Wait, there's one gift left to give," called out Hannah Somme. "Mister P'Thok, I checked the tag, it's for you."

P'Thok turned and looked, wondering who had left him a gift, question marks appearing over his head.

It was a shining glittering ball, swirling stars and dancing specks.

"Take it, P'Thok," Windy-Wu yawned. "It's made just for you."

"You should have a Happy New Year too," said the Grunch, smiling with yellow teeth.

P'Thok touched the ball and everything whirled.

"Merry Christmas and Happy New Year!" cried out his new friends.

With a flash P'Thok appeared back in deep space. His helmet and spacesuit back in their place. He turned around slowly, looking around, but no trace of Windy-Wu or the Grunch did he found.

He saw his own ship, the crew waiting with fear, but P'Thok wasn't afraid, his ship was quite near.

Using thrusters that jingled out a tune while the flames were different hued, P'Thok made his way back to his spaceship to the relief of the crew.

Once aboard the ship, P'Thok shook his head. Surely what he'd seen had been a dream instead.

But as he took off his helmet from his head fell a clue.

A Santa hat that said it was all true.

>MANTID FREE WORLD CLAPS

TNVARU GRIPPING HANDS

So, did it happen or not?

---NOTHING FOLLOWS---

TREANA'AD HIVE WORLDS

It happened and we'll fight anyone who says otherwise.

---NOTHING FOLLOWS---

TNVARU GRIPPING HANDS

All right, all right, no need to get excited.

---NOTHING FOLLOWS---

>MANTID SNIFFS AND WIPES A TEAR

MANTID FREE WORLDS

Merry Christmas and a Happy New Year.

DON'T BE "THAT GUY"

(Approx. 8,000 Terran Years after the P'Thok Liberation)

T'Nok was born a warrior caste male. As large as a Terran warborg at just over three meters, his blade arms were thick and highly honed, his gripping hands were strong, and his legs were thick and powerful. Before the P'Thok Liberation he would have undoubtedly been eaten during his first mating, his coloration and physique and intellect making him highly desirable. His cranium was well developed and his school scores put him at the top of his classes. The tattoo on his abdomen from the Bongistan University of Lumbering Meat Beast Water Crossing was a source of pride for him and his sash proclaimed to every female and male who saw him that he was not only a prime physical specimen but his intellect made him highly desirable. The fact that he was a reknown crysteel architect made him wealthy and highly sought after to grow the elaborate living crystal domiciles the higher caste females so preferred. More than a females would see him and clean their bladearms while they stared at him.

Which was why he was glad that birth control and ice cream was a thing. He liked his head.

He had been designing a particularly challenging birthing chamber for a shipping company matron and decided to go out and enjoy a bowl of ice cream, perhaps even a banana split, to relax and sweep load bearing computations from his mind. On the trip in his comfortable travel-disc he loaded his favorite game and spent time arranging coins just right for a virtual Terran monkey to grab as it bounced off of walls and objects. It helped discharge the formula from his datalink implant and reset his nervous system.

The ice cream parlor that he preferred was high end and upscale. The bench seats were made of red dyed moomoo skins in an arcane process that produced soft but firm red leather. All of the edges of surfaces were made of chrome. Each table had a delightful radio that ensured that those sitting at the booths could listen to old style Treana'ad music as the waitresses, wearing large wigs and elaborate white costumes, would roll around on the skates on all four of their legs. He liked the coloration of the ice cream artist working that day, her skill with carving ice cream floats with her sterilized bladearms made him hum in satisfaction.

The sight of the backdrop, showing a Treana'ad on a long board, balancing with an ice cream cone in one hand and a cigarette on the other, as he used the board to skim along the inside of an ocean wave, reminded him that he was going to go foot-disc or foot-board surfing with some friends next week. He double-checked his implant to make sure the appointment was locked in. His friends had all certified their RSVP's and while he waited for the waitress he made sure to order high quality bonfire wood, special order ice cream, and actual Terran Dark Continent Wonderbeast steaks to cook over the open flame.

The waitress took his order, a rainbow tower of sherbet, left him a complimentary cigarette and book of matches, and skated away, tapping her bladearms together in tune with the jaunty song that was playing.

"Hey, T'Nok," came a voice.

Crap, it's J'Vik, T'Nok thought to himself. He found the other Treana'ad somewhat boorish, with poor taste in ice-cream and worse taste in poetry that he tried to inflict upon everyone around him. The problem was, like T'Nok, J'Vik was warrior-caste born, which meant that T'Nok had to be at least polite to him in public. Only J'Vik fancied himself a 'warrior poet' and suffered a fundamental misunderstanding of what that actually meant.

T'Nok looked up and saw that J'Vik was wearing a beatnik on his head. One of those flattened hats the humans called berets. Which T'Nok thought was funny, since the phonetic sounds of 'beret' meant 'delicious looking' in his native language.

Only J'Vik would walk around proclaiming that his head looked delicious with his hat, T'Nok mused, managing to keep from laughing by lighting a cigarette.

The other male sat down and T'Nok made a mental bet with himself that the other male would try to stick T'Nok with the tab.

"Did you hear the news? Everyone is talking about it," J'Vik said, completely unaware of the three barely mature females in the next booth over snickering about his hat and wondering if his head was as delicious as J'Vik was claiming. All three of them had the shiny carapaces of someone who had molted within the last week.

Two of them were wondering if they should lure the 'warrior poet' back to their nests, share him, and then discuss on the satisfaction they got from the taste, consistency, and volume of J'Vik's head.

T'Nok calmed his anxiety over the three females, who would undoubtedly eat a male's head, birth control or no birth control, just because their just matured primal instinct told them too, and enjoy a nice bowl of chocolate fudge cheesecake ripple afterwards.

Barely mature females were dangerous, everyone knew that, but there was always 'That Guy' who thought that his head was armor plated.

All of his life T'Nok had been careful not to be 'That Guy'. He'd known a few.

J'Vik definitely fell in the "That Guy" category.

"I have been busy with my work. My client is most eager for me to complete my work," T'Nok said, exhaling smoke through his forward legs.

"Got a smoke?" J'Vik asked.

"Alas, I did not bring a pack along. Perhaps when you order?" T'Nok said.

"Here, I have one," one of the females said, leaning over the back of the bench and offering a menthol cigarette. "You can have it," she said, staring at J'Vik's beatnik.

The other two slowly cleaned their bladearms with their mandibles, their compound eyes sparkling as they watched their friend offer the cigarette.

"Thank you, pretty," J'Vik said, fluttering his antenna at the female.

She turned around with a titter and rubbing her wings together, looking smugly at her two companions, as J'Vik lit the menthol.

Don't be That Guy, T'Nok thought to himself.

"I'm surprised you didn't hear. It's pretty big news, especially for your caste," J'Vik said somewhat smugly.

"You are too concerned with castes," T'Nok said, shaking his head. "We are free of castes."

"Mm-hmm,' J'Vik said, making T'Nok want to roll his eyes but his eyes weren't designed in such a way. "Easy for you to say."

J'Vik preened for a moment.

Oh, warrior, who has everything he pleases
Cannot I have a bowl that you have not cleaned
For I am but a worker
In this society of ours

J'Vik said. He preened for a moment, ignorant of the giggling of the three females and the flat out laughter from two matrons watching over a clutch of a dozen little hatchlings.

"I wrote that," J'Vik said.

"You're not worker caste," T'Nok reminded him.

"Poetry transcends caste," J'Vik said, smugly cleaning his antenna with his bladearms.

T'Nok tapped his bladearms in a shrug. "I am not one for poetry," T'Nok said. Not quite true, he quite enjoyed Hard Core Rigellian Saurian Gangster Rap. He particularly enjoyed the recent poetry-song 'I got yer eggs right here, suckah' by the Big Tail Ganstas.

"Your caste often is not," J'Vik said. "Still, I would have thought that you would be excited by the news."

T'Nok gave a sigh. "What news?"

"The Confederacy voted to go to war this morning," J'Vik said, excitement in his voice.

T'Nok froze. He had to close his opaque eye-shields for moment as the horror rolled through his mind. History requirements in school had ensured he'd been exposed to plenty of media he would have preferred to avoid.

Only someone like J'Vik would be happy that uncounted sentient beings will kill each other, he thought to himself.

"You're excited, I can tell," J'Vik said. "I knew that news would speak to you and excite you."

"Have you ever been to TerraSol?" T'Nok asked carefully. He signaled one of the waitresses to bring him a pack of smokes, changed his mind, and asked for a powersmoker, a 'vape' as the humans called it along with a swamp-apple flavored cartridge.

J'Vik gripped his hands together in a frown. "Why? Oh, because the Terrans will undoubtedly be fighting in the war?"

T'Nok had to resist the urge to hold the smaller male down and allow the three females to eat his head.

"I take it you'll be signing up right away?" J'Vik asked.

T'Nok managed not to sigh, turning and thanking the waitress for the power-smoker and tipping her a handful of credits for her ability not to snicker at J'Vik's beatnik.

"Why would I do that? I don't know one end of a power-rifle from the other," T'Nok said, shrugging again. "I'm sure the Confederate Military can get along just fine without me dropping my rifle and accidentally shooting off my own genitals."

That made the three girls snicker as they slowly cleaned/sharpened their bladearms, still staring at J'Vik's hat.

"But the Confederacy is going to war," J'Vik actually sounded confused that T'Nok hadn't jumped up, ran out into the parking lot, and immediately fired off a power-rifle into the air.

"Which is a profession and activity best left to skilled professionals," T'Nok shrugged. "The closest I've been to warfare is I watched the episode of The Nitrogen Seven when they robbed the Terran Army base only to discover that they'd just stolen a bunch of Terran pornographic magazines instead of the Commander's secret ice cream recipe, and that series is a Tri-Vid comedy."

"Well," J'Vik preened with smugness for a moment. "I heard they're going to start a draft. I'm sure such a prime specimen of the warrior caste such as yourself will be right at the top of the list."

T'Nok shook his head. "A draft is as likely as," he stopped himself from saying 'You writing decent poetry' and instead got out "the Digital Omnimessiah appearing in the bathroom to bless the faucets."

The females giggled to each other.

"It's all the talk on the Net Boards," J'Vik said.

"I would suggest not spending so much time on the Boards," T'Nok scoffed. "Just last week you were telling me that there was going to be a chocolate shortage by now, but here we are and the prices are the same."

"Peak chocolate is real," J'Vik said, straightening up, his wings rubbing in anxiety.

"Pfft, you sound like a Precursor," T'Nok said. "There is only enough chocolate for me."

The girls snickered again.

"Well, of course, you wouldn't notice any shortages. Your caste never does," J'Vik said.

T'Nok took a long pull off of the power-smoker and exhaled through his legs, feeling irritation rise up.

If we were still having castes, I'd tear your bladearms off by now, he thought to himself. *No, not my education, not my years of study and hard work even sacrificing social gatherings, but no, it's all my caste, all my coloration and size. It doesn't even matter we're the same caste to you.*

"Hmmph, you're feeling annoyed because you know I'm right," J'Vik said, his antenna flicking with smug assurance.

"You realize you're warrior caste too," T'Nok pointed out. He didn't point out that J'Vik would have been eaten as a hatchling if the caste system was still in place.

J'Vik might have been warrior caste but his coloration was poor, he was small for a male, and his vestigial wings were off pitch when he rubbed them. Worse than that, his poetry was execrable and he had put off education to create poetry and live off of his parent's wealth.

That made J'Vik sit quietly for a moment. The waitress came by and J'Vik ordered a triple chocolate destructor bomb with double-fudge.

She didn't leave a complimentary cigarette and T'Nok almost busted out laughing.

"When are you signing up for the war?" J'Vik said once both of their ice cream had been delivered. The three barely mature females had ordered half-bowls and were giggled to each other, still eyeing J'Vik's head. J'Vik, of course, started eating his ice cream like it was going to vanish while T'Nok savored his, letting it partially melt and mix properly.

"Never. Me joining the military would be suspected of an enemy plot," T'Nok answered. "I would be so incompetent as a warrior they would suspect me to be an enemy agent."

"I figured you'd be braver," J'Vik said, pushing his empty bowl away. "Where's your caste pride?"

That made T'Nok sit up straight, reaching for the power-smoker to mask his pheromones of anger. "Don't go there, J'Vik. You and I are the same birth-caste, but that does not give you the right to insult me."

"Insult is never given only taken," J'Vik quoted, sounding smug. "I thought a prime example of the warrior caste such as yourself would be more inured against perceived insults."

Really? Quoting Terran stoicism at me? Well, let's see about that. I've about had it with your subtle insults, T'Nok thought, not bothering to pick up the power-smoker in order to let the other male realize how angry T'Nok was.

"J'Vik, if you feel your ability to attract mates is so threatened by my very existence to the point of attempting to goad me into joining a profession I would be incompetent at, in hopes I would be killed in some far off struggle, then perhaps you should attempt to reconcile that with the obvious issue that you are too cowardly to sign up to go to war despite being warrior caste yourself," T'Nok said, tapping the edge of his spoon on the bowl.

Every female in the ice cream parlor, even the waitresses, burst out laughing. The high pitched squeals, the humming of wings, even the chirping of matrons rubbing their back legs together filled the parlor.

J'Vik went completely still.

Finish him! T'Nok heard in his mind and he tapped his ice cream bowl with a bladearm tip making it ring as he continued speaking, delivering the final bladearm thrust.

"I'm sure if the enemy attacks you can drive them off with that detestable whining you insist is poetry that you instead inflict upon us all every time you see another male that appears to be content with his own life due to the glorious fact that he is not you," T'Nok finished.

Even the other males joined in with the laughter.

"Ice pack for table nine to treat that burn!" A male called out.

"Confederate statutes don't allow you to own someone like that!" a female laughed.

"Quick, molt your shell and run off before he realizes your husk isn't you!" another female giggled.

Someone threw the image of J'Vik up on the ice cream parlor's display with the caption "LOCAL MALE MURDERED BY WORDS" underneath. The image of J'Vik looked up as a shadow covered him just in time to be crushed by the words "U R PO-EHT!"

J'Vik didn't move the entire time, pheromones of anger rolling off of him.

The three barely mature females sniffed the air and perked up, clicking their mandibles and rubbing their bladearms together in excitement. One dipped the tip of her bladearm in the ice cream in front of her and carefully cleaned it as she stared at J'Vik's head.

When the laughter died J'Vik slowly looked around, then back at T'Nok.

"You're caste..." he started loudly.

"We're the same birth-caste, J'Vik," T'Nok answered slightly louder. T'Nok held up his gripping hands and flexed his fingers.

"Insult is only taken never given," T'Nok quoted back.

"How dare you insult me in such a manner," J'Vik said. "That quote is not meant for someone intentionally insulting someone the way you have."

"Put up," T'Nok said, raising his gripping hands and flexed his fingers. He flexed his wrists. "Or shut up," T'Nok finished.

J'Vik clattered out of the booth. "A Gripping Hand Challenge it is, then, T'Nok. In the parking lot. Right now."

"Traditionally I would choose the location," T'Nok said, moving out of the bench seat. "But that's fine with me."

J'Vik was opening and closing his gripping hands, obviously trying to impress everyone with his grip.

The matrons, mature females, and the three just mature females all hurried out of the ice-cream parlor with almost unseemly haste. The mixing of anger pheromones of two males making the veins in their wings flush with blood.

Even the waitresses and ice cream sculptors came out.

The males of course, hung back. Not wanting to get involved.

A matron, a half-dozen small hatchlings hanging on her abdomen, moved forward with grace and elegance. She sniffed at the air, tasting the anger pheromones in the air.

"Can this only be settled by challenge and not a cigarette and conversation?" She asked. "Perhaps a cigarette or two will mask the scent of your anger and allow you to discuss your emotions with more cultural maturity than you are feeling now?"

"If J'Vik wishes to submit I will accept," T'Nok said, looming over the smaller warrior-caste male.

Several of the females breathed deep.

"Insulted I have been

"Words cutting most cruel

"I will not remain

"Insulted without response," J'Vik quoted poetry that made several of the females snicker. He looked around almost smugly. "I created that."

More giggles and J'Vik went rigid.

"Gripping hand challenge it is," the matron said. The little ones one her back raised up their bladearms in joy, their immature minds reacting to the angry pheromones in the air.

One had ice-cream on his head, between his eyes.

T'Nok held still as J'Vik moved into position. They locked hands, interlacing fingers. Their bladearms clashed, held away from each other's bodies and pointed away from one another.

The matron lifted up a handkerchief and waved it between the two males.

Several cars had stopped to watch. Challenges were exciting to witness. They were less common over the last few centuries, but still occurred with enough frequency that they could not be outlawed.

The handkerchief fell from her hand and danced away on the breeze. The larger of the three just-mature females hurried over and picked it up, bringing it to her face and inhaling deeply as she moved back over to her friends and passed it to the next biggest one.

T'Nok didn't notice. He just locked his wrists and tensed his fingers as he pushed out and down with his bladearms.

Your grip is nothing. I used to play this with my drunk Terram frat-brothers in Bongistan, T'Nok thought to himself as the other male squeezed tightly, attempted to twist T'Nok's wrists backward, and pushed ineffectively with his bladearms.

Getting a Doctorate in Architectural Engineering with a minor in Materials Science had required over a decade of study, and during that time T'Nok had tempered his natural aggressiveness by socializing with his Terran Descent Human school mates.

A matron tittered as J'Vik had to open his wings slightly to breathe as he kept struggling to move T'Nok's wrists or bladearms.

"Yield," T'Nok ordered. The sun was shimmering down, warming him, and the sweetness of the day's nitrogen level gave him strength.

"No," J'Vik's feet ground against the tarmac as he attempted to lean into the gripping contest. The way his back feet scrabbled on the pavement made several females giggle and the smell of his anger increased.

T'Nok began to bring his hands forward, squeezing tightly.

He knew that J'Vik had figured that T'Nok's grip would be weak, that T'Nok spent his days working with architecture and computer programs.

T'Nok also shaped the crystal of his creations with his own hands rather than robots. The tiny imperfections is what gave his works their beauty.

J'Vik's hands began to bend back and his bladearms were forced down and outward to the point of pain and still T'Nok just stared at the other male as he increased the pressure.

J'Vik's legs gave out and he crashed to the ground, giving a high keen of pain. T'Nok released his hands and stepped back as J'Vik moaned and lifted his hands and arms protectively against his thorax. The thick sour smell of defeat emanated from defeated male.

The matron stepped forward, an ornate and bejeweled power-smoker held up to her mandibles with one beringed hand as she inhaled deeply and expelled smoke from her legs and abdomen. The smoke covered the two males, wiping away the smell of anger, contention, and defeat.

"Thank you, your grace," T'Nok told the wealthy matron.

"Of course," she replied. The little ones on her abdomen raised their bladearms and gave small shrieks of victory to him.

"And thank you, little ones," T'Nok said.

The three just matured females, their just-molted carapaces shining and glittering in the sun, rushed forward to comfort J'Vik.

The gathered Treana'ad moved back into the ice cream parlor, gossiping about what they'd just seen, many of them showing one another the recordings they'd made of the contest, admiring one another's angles or artistic filters.

T'Nok was thinking. He had been struggling with nitrogen release in the garden of the birthing chamber. Enough to encourage the eggs to hatch and the grubs to mature, but not exposing it to the air or depend too much on computerized systems.

Tantervellian ferns. They uptake, fix, and release nitrogen on a steady pattern, he mused as he returned to his table.

The ice cream parlor's central air system had cleared away the heavy pheromones of anger and T'Nok sat down, moving the holo-emitter from next to the radio to the center of the table. He transferred his planning file to the holo-emitter and idly moved things around with one bladearm as he slowly ate and savored his ice cream.

J'Vik left with the three females, who were comforting and praising him. One of them had a fancy hover-disc, painted bright attention getting hyper-blue with ultra-violet accents. All four of them sat on the

P'THOK CHRONICLES

comfortable seats and the bigger female activated the privacy screen as the hover-disc floated away.

Paying attention to his work, T'Nok didn't notice J'Vik leaving or the interested looks from the females. He went through another bowl before he was finished, leaning back and looking at the chamber. The ferns provided just the right edging. The grubs, which would burrow under the ground and eat roots, would avoid the ferns due to dirt, sticking to the sand of the middle of the chamber.

It would give the chamber the right nitrogen cycle in the right levels without requiring HVAC systems that the matron was concerned might harm her grubs.

On the way home, relaxing in his hover-disc, one of the public warning billboards caught his eye.

J'Vik was featured prominently.

Below him a scrolling banner read: "UNCONTROLLED EMOTIONS KILL! DON'T LOSE YOUR HEAD LIKE HE DID! 836 LOST IN THIS CITY THIS WEEK ALONE! SMOKING SAVES LIVES!"

Right as he passed the huge sign a stamp appeared across J'Vik.

"DON'T BE THAT GUY!"

T'Nok laughed all the way home.

Made in the USA
Monee, IL
09 January 2021